I Wanted to Remember

Prologue

Larry and I had the perfect life. We started dating when we were fifteen. We married when we were both twenty-four and had two beautiful daughters, Carolyn and Cindy. Carolyn was always the dominant of the two, or should I say bossy, and Cindy was more of the tag-a-long, always just going along with whatever Carolyn said. But they were very close growing up, since they were only two years apart.

The four of us were a very close-knit family, and the girls were both daddy's girls. Larry worked full-time, I was a stay-at-home mom, and the girls went to school. We went to church on Sundays. Larry provided us with everything we needed. We had a large house in the suburbs of Bedford Hills, Michigan, and never wanted for anything. We were quite fortunate back in those days.

Larry and I would often take the girls on vacations, to Florida, Washington D.C., Arizona, and so on. We took them all over the country. It was important to us that they explore and see different ways of life. If we could have afforded to take them outside of the country, we would have. But living in little Bedford Hills, we wanted them to get out and see what other areas of the country had to offer.

Larry never made a big fuss if one of the girls acted up. I tended to get a little heated, but he was always pretty mellow. One thing he always told me was the old adage, "This too shall pass." And he was right. He was almost always right. I should have listened to him more back then, as those days passed us by many years ago.

One thing we tried to do on a weekly basis was have a family game night. It didn't matter how busy we were or what excuses the girls came up with, we still made time for our family game night. We had a whole drawer in the dining room cabinet full of board games that we took turns choosing from and played for hours. Larry got a kick out of that. That's one thing I hope the girls will always remember.

Larry was a good father and a good husband. I miss him.

Chapter 1

People tend to think that us older folks don't grieve as much when our loved ones pass away, as if our feelings harden as we grow older like frosting on a forgotten piece of cake. I only wish that were true. My husband, Larry, is—was the love of my life. The day he passed away was the beginning of a new life for me, and not one that I wanted. But let me back up a bit.

Larry's funeral was beautiful. So many people came from all over town, and even from surrounding towns. Everyone knew Larry, as he was a traveling salesman for many years before taking a job at a local insurance company before his retirement. People were drawn to his outgoing personality and fun-loving spirit. When Larry died suddenly of a heart attack, I wasn't the only one who was devastated. There were so many flowers and a huge outpouring of love at the viewing and funeral.

People asked me how I was holding up, but I could tell they expected me to be okay. My daughters stood by my side and they never wavered a bit, strong as rocks. I felt I had to be the same, for their sakes. To tell the truth, I was starting to get a bit overwhelmed with the whole thing. My husband of fifty-four years was gone. He was never coming back. I was never going to see him again after the burial. At times, I could barely remain standing as people walked through the line.

After the funeral, my daughters, Carolyn and Cindy, brought me back to the house that my husband and I had shared. That's when they dropped the bomb on me, right after the funeral.

"Mom, there's something we need to talk about," Cindy said.

"Okay," I replied.

"We're worried about you," she answered.

"How so?" I asked.

"We're worried about you here without Dad," Carolyn said. "He did a lot for you."

"What do you mean?" I asked. I had a bad feeling where this conversation was going.

"Mom, he took care of all of the finances, he did all of the cooking because of that time you left the stove on. He did all of the driving. These are just a few of the reasons why we're worried about you trying to stay by yourself here at home," Cindy said.

"I know my vision is poor, and I've made some mistakes," I said. "But I can't possibly ask to come live with one of you."

The two of them glanced at one another.

"That's not exactly what we were thinking," Cindy said.

"We were thinking we could take a trip up to Pine Meadows and just take a look around, see if that might be a good fit for you," Carolyn said, nonchalantly.

I gasped, "Are you kidding me? Your father just died, we just buried him, and now you want to put me in a nursing home? I can't believe you two. I can't believe you won't even consider just giving me a chance to make it on my own here."

"Mother, it's not like we're moving you in tonight," Carolyn said, "We don't even know if it would be the right fit for you anyway. Maybe you would be okay here at home. We're just concerned and we'd like to schedule a visit to Pine Meadows just to see what the place looks like and what they have to offer. Is that fair?"

Not really, I wanted to say. "Okay, I suppose so," I replied. I didn't feel I had much choice in the matter.

Carolyn and Cindy stuck around long enough to make sure I got settled in and then left to attend to their own families. I was alone in our house, Larry's and my house, for the first night in a very long time. Larry had been away on business trips before, but that was several years ago. Recently, he had been home every night. I was lonely.

I was also tired. I wanted to go upstairs to our bedroom and go to sleep. As I headed toward the staircase, I realized I was too tired to take the first step up. That had never happened before. It must have been from too much standing and from all of the day's events. I decided I would make a night of it, sleeping on the couch in my funeral clothes. At least I would get some rest.

The next morning, I woke to the doorbell ringing. Lethargic state, I went to the door to see who it was—Carolyn.

"Mom, what are you doing wearing the same clothes as yesterday?"

"I was too tired to change," I said.

"Well, go upstairs and change clothes really quick. We're going to Pine Meadows today," she said.

"I can't," I replied.

"What do you mean you can't?"

"I can't get up the stairs. I think I stood too much at the viewing or the funeral wore me out. I tried getting up the stairs last night and I just couldn't."

"You can't get up the stairs to your own bedroom?" Carolyn asked in disbelief.

"Not as of last night, but I think it will wear off. I might be able to today," I said.

"Go try," she said.

So, I went to the staircase again. This time I was determined to make it up those steps. With my lithe frame, it should have been no problem. I grabbed hold of the handrail and lifted one foot up onto the first step. With all of my might, I tried to hoist my body up onto that step with my second foot, but I wasn't able. Carolyn just shook her head.

"I don't know what we're going to do mother. If you're going to stay here, we're going to have to install a stair lift, or we're going to have to find a place to put a bed downstairs. Either option is not ideal. And your bathroom is upstairs! How are you going to take a shower?" Carolyn said.

"There's no place to put a bed downstairs," I replied, "I'll be able to make it up those steps. I just did it a couple of days ago. I'm just tired. And there's a half bath down here. I can sponge bathe for now. Why don't you just bring down a few changes of clothes for me and I'll sleep on the sofa for a couple of nights until I feel better?"

"I'm going to go get you a change of clothes now so that we can go visit Pine Meadows, but we'll have to address this issue later. I want to talk this over with Cindy."

While Carolyn was upstairs picking out a change of clothes for me, I couldn't help but just feel ashamed. I used to pick out clothes for my daughter and now she had to do that for me. I felt like the least I could do was make us each a cup of coffee before we left for what was bound to be a depressing visit to Pine Meadows.

I filled the carafe with water and added it to the coffee maker, then added the coffee grounds to the filter. I turned the coffee pot on and let the kitchen fill with the sweet aroma of coffee brewing. As soon as it was done, I got out two mugs and began to pour the coffee. However, as I was pouring my cup, the coffee pot slipped in my hand, and I poured the hot coffee onto my other hand, the one that was holding the mug. I yelped, dropped the coffee pot, and immediately stuck my burned hand under cold water.

Carolyn must have heard the yelp as she came running down the stairs to see what the commotion was all about.

"Oh, Mother, what happened?" she cried.

"Nothing. It's nothing, really," I said.

"It doesn't look like nothing to me," Carolyn sighed as she picked up the coffee pot off of the floor and got some paper towels to soak up the leftover coffee from the carpet.

"I burned my hand and dropped the coffee pot," I said. "But I'm fine, really."

"Let's take a look at your hand," Carolyn said.

I pulled my hand out from under the faucet. It was bright red and starting to bubble a little.

"I think we need to cancel our trip to Pine Meadows today and take you to the doctor," Carolyn said, "And I'm going to call Cindy to come along."

Chapter 2

Luckily, or maybe not so luckily, Dr. Stanbery was able to get me in to be seen that same day. I suppose it helped when Carolyn called, frantically telling the receptionist that I had burned myself. So, I changed into the clothes that Carolyn brought downstairs for me, then Carolyn, Cindy, and I traveled to the doctor's office for my visit.

When I arrived, we had to wait our obligatory forty-five minutes in the waiting room, until finally a nurse called us back. The doctor came in not much later and examined my hand. He bandaged it and said it was a second-degree burn. He gave Carolyn and Cindy extra supplies and made sure they understood how to re-bandage the dressing every twenty-four hours until it was healed. At this point, I assumed the appointment was over, but my daughters had other plans.

"Doctor Stanbery, we're concerned about our mother trying to live on her own at home. She has low vision, she can't drive, she doesn't cook, and just recently she hasn't been able to make it up the stairs to her own bedroom and bathroom, and now this incident with burning her hand with hot coffee has happened. We're wondering what are your thoughts on her going to live in a nursing home?" Carolyn asked.

"Well, I can tell you that's not necessarily up to me," Dr. Stanbery said. "However, given the nature of what you're telling me, it sounds like she is having a difficult time living at home alone and that it will probably only get more difficult as time goes on. There are many nursing homes out there that are wonderful facilities that provide excellent care that would be the optimal environment for Judith."

"So, you think it would be wise for us to pursue this?" Carolyn asked.

"I don't think it would be out of the question," Dr. Stanbery said.

"Don't I get a say in any of this?" I asked, exasperated.

"Of course you do, Judith," Dr. Stanbery said, "But please remember, you and Larry made Carolyn your Healthcare Power of Attorney several years back, which means that if she feels you are unsafe in your home, she can decide that you would be better fit in a nursing home."

I immediately regretted that decision. At the time, I was only thinking that if something happened to one of us and the other was on life support or something, Carolyn could make the decision to pull the plug or make the decision to make one of us a Do-Not-Resuscitate if we were in really bad shape. Never in my mind did I think I was giving her permission to put me in a nursing home, especially at a time like this, not right after my husband passed away.

When we left that appointment, I was feeling pretty down. Not only did my hand hurt, but so did my pride. If I kept making mistakes at home, my daughters were sure to put me in Pine Meadows or some other facility. And now, I was one handed, could barely see, confined to the first floor of my home, with no husband to help me. Maybe I did belong in Pine Meadows.

Chapter 3

Carolyn, Cindy, and I arrived at Pine Meadows around eleven o'clock, just around the time the residents were eating lunch. The nursing home administrator said that was just perfect, because we could see the dining room full of people. I had to admit, the dining room did look impressive. One whole wall was made up of large windows that looked out over a garden of beautiful flowers that the administrator said the residents planted in the spring. As an avid gardener, that did pique my interest, slightly.

A group of women who appeared to be around my age sat together at a large table, toward the front of the dining room. A couple of them waved hello. I waved back as a nice gesture. At the very least, I had the peace of mind of knowing that a couple of these people were friendly, should I end up here.

The administrator then took us to the activity room. She said that their facility had a top-notch activities program and often took residents for outings out of the facility in the facility's handicap-accessible van. Cindy thought that was just fantastic.

"Where all do you usually go?" she asked.

"We often take trips to Wal-mart, trips out to eat at local restaurants, and occasionally out to minor league baseball and hockey games," the administrator smiled.

"That sounds wonderful, doesn't it Mom?" Cindy prodded.

"Yes, it does sound nice," I said. And, it did. I knew with Larry being gone, I would have a difficult time getting out and about on my own due to my reduced vision and inability to drive. I didn't want to have to rely on Carolyn and Cindy to have to take me places every time I needed something. However, I didn't want to have to live in a nursing home, losing my independence, in order to maintain this small level of independence. It made no sense.

Joanna, the nursing home administrator, took us then on a tour of the rooms. Each room was private; however, the bathrooms were shared with a roommate on the other side of a double curtain. There was no shower in the room. There was a community shower by the nurses' station and each resident was scheduled for two to three showers per week, with the help of a nursing assistant. Joanna also explained that they had a strict policy at the facility that no one was to get up without using their call button, which was a small button on a cord in each room. The call button alerted the staff that the resident was in need of something. In turn, the staff would come to the resident's door and ask what he or she needed. If the resident needed to get up for any reason, whether it was to go from the chair to the bed or go to the bathroom, the staff member was to assist that resident at all times. She explained that this was only for residents' safety, as they did not want any of their residents to experience a fall or injury.

Carolyn and Cindy didn't say much when it came to this topic. I didn't say too much either. I wasn't keen on the idea at all, and planned to discuss it with them after the tour was over. Joanna was starting to make Pine Meadows sound like more like a prison than a care facility.

Joanna also gave us a tour of the therapy area, where residents could utilize exercise equipment under the supervision of a therapist; the day area, which included a small library and a television, as well as some board games; and an area in one of the hallways that contained a large aquarium full of fish that the residents could watch at their leisure.

At the end of the tour, Joanna asked if any of us had any questions about Pine Meadows or if she could assist us further in any way.

"I have a question," I said. "If I come to live here, can I ever leave?"

"Do you mean leave for good? Or do you mean leave for a short period of time?"

"Well, I guess, both," I said.

"You can certainly leave for a temporary leave of absence if your daughter signs you out and Dr. Stanbery signs an order stating that he is okay with it. As far as leaving for good, that would be entirely up to Carolyn."

I sighed. I felt like I was on trial. I had no further questions.

"Is there any way Mom could get more than two to three showers per week? She's used to bathing every day." Cindy asked.

"We would certainly do our best to make that happen," Joanna said.

"Who does her laundry?" Carolyn asked, "Do we take it home and do it? Or do you do her laundry here?"

"That can be done either way. If we do the laundry here, we just ask for an extra small fee. You are welcome to take her laundry home and do it yourselves if you wish to save a couple dollars."

"What's the current ratio of residents to nursing assistants?" Carolyn asked.

Boy, she was getting a little feisty. Despite what she was doing to me, I was a little proud of my daughter. She was looking out for me in her own way.

"Right now, it's variable." Joanna said, "But our average is approximately eight residents per nursing assistant."

"That seems a bit high," Cindy said, her forehead wrinkling.

"I assure you, we are currently hiring, and our nurses do chip in and help answer call lights as needed. Your mother will be well taken care of here at Pine Meadows," Joanna said.

There was a long pause after that.

"Does anyone have any other questions?" Joanna asked.

"No, I think we're all set," Carolyn said.

When we arrived home, Carolyn and Cindy argued over which one was going to spend the night with me. Without knowing it, I was no longer allowed to live in my own home alone. It was Carolyn who came out on top, as she usually did since she was the older of the two. Cindy said her goodbyes and promised she would be back in the morning to check in and make sure everything was okay on her way to run errands.

Carolyn wanted to chat about the day's visit at Pine Meadows.

"What did you think, Mom? Honestly?"

"Honestly? I think I'd never want to live there," I said.

"Mother, I'll be brutally honest with you, I've done the research. Not only is Pine Meadows the closest nursing home to both Cindy and I, it's also got the highest rating of all the other nursing homes in the area. I didn't tell you this earlier, because I didn't want to upset you, but Cindy and I went to visit a few of the other local nursing homes and they were not good. Pine Meadows is a palace compared to those other facilities. If you really want to, we can set up another tour at some of those places and take you with us, just so you can see—"

"No, that's quite alright," I interrupted. I don't usually interrupt, but I was fed up. All of these plans had been made behind my back, and apparently even before Larry had passed away. I felt the tears stinging in my eyes. I hadn't cried in front of my daughter since the day she was born. I looked around my home, *my home,* and felt such a sense of loss. Not only had I just lost my husband, the love of my life, I was also going to lose our home where we made all of our memories too. The tears started flowing. A seventy-eight-year-old woman can still cry, believe it or not.

Chapter 4

It was difficult packing things up to move in to Pine Meadows. There was only so much I could take to fit in such a small room. It was especially difficult that I couldn't get upstairs to the bedroom and had to rely on the girls to bring things down and determine if it was to go or stay. The girls were exhausted bringing things up and down the stairs, and didn't hesitate to let it show.

Two small suitcases and a compact case contained all of my future belongings by the time we were done packing everything up. It was depressing. I looked around the house at everything I was leaving behind. I realized I was leaving everything of Larry's at the house, to potentially be sold at auction. I needed to have something of his with me. I asked Carolyn for his pocket watch.

"Sure, Mother," she said, as she went back upstairs to get it from the bedroom closet.

Cindy gave me a hug, "Everything is going to be okay, Mom. You're doing the right thing."

Carolyn came back downstairs with the pocket watch and placed it inside the front pocket of one of my suitcases.

"You girls aren't planning on selling the house right away, are you?" I asked.

"Why do you ask?" Carolyn replied.

"Because I would really like this whole ordeal to be on a trial basis," I said. "I'll do therapy at Pine Meadows and anything else they ask me to do, and if I get better, I'd like to be able to come back home."

"I think that's a fair compromise," Carolyn said, "with the exception that we would try home on a trial basis as well if that were to occur."

"Okay, it's a deal," I said. I had my first glimmer of hope in days.

"It's time for us to get some rest, Mother," Cindy said, as she was the one staying with me that night. "We have a big day tomorrow."

We had a big day indeed. As soon as Carolyn met us in the morning, we loaded up the car and headed to Pine Meadows. The car ride was dreadful. I felt like I was going to vomit the entire way. When we pulled up to the front entrance, instead of the picturesque landscape and beautiful hand-crafted benches sitting outside, I couldn't help but conjure up the image of a prison, knowing that inside there were little tiny cells with a button I had to press before I could move.

As we walked in, Joanna greeted us at the door right away. She explained that one of the nursing assistants would show us to my room and would be with us shortly. We sat down on a bench to wait. Approximately twenty-five minutes later, a young girl—who appeared to be in her late teens—arrived and said her name was Kristi. She said she would be showing me to my room.

Kristi asked if I needed a wheelchair, walker, or a cane for the distance, to which I replied no. She still acted apprehensive and stayed close to my side the entire time, as if she was afraid I was going to fall. Kristi explained that I would be in room 422-A and that my roommate on the other side of the bathroom's name was Anna.

As we arrived at 422-A, it was quite a trek from the main hub of the nurses' station, activities room, dining hall, and therapy gym. I considered this a good thing, as I could really get my exercise in walking to and from these areas every day. However, the first thing I noticed inside room 422-A was a wheelchair.

"I don't need that," I said to Kristi, pointing at the wheelchair.

"Every room has one," she said.

"But I don't need it. I can walk," I said.

My daughters chimed in.

"She really can walk. You saw her walk down here," Carolyn said.

"She doesn't need a wheelchair. It would be better to give to someone who truly needs it," Cindy said.

"I don't really have a choice," Kristi said, "I have to follow the rules, and the rules state that every room has to have a wheelchair."

The three of us just let it go at that. It would be one more thing taking up valuable space in my tiny room, and I didn't like that.

All at once, multiple bells started ringing in the hallway.

"I've got to go answer those lights," Kristi said. "I'll let you all get settled in. Press your call light if you need anything." And she left.

The three of us just looked at each other.

"I guess we better start unpacking," I said.

It didn't take long for us to fill the dresser and tiny nightstand with all of my things. We hung family photos on the wall, photos of Larry and I from the past as well as photos of Carolyn and Cindy and their families. I especially wanted photos of my grandchildren. They used to come visit Larry and me quite a bit at the house. I could only hope they'd do the same for me at Pine Meadows. We put Larry's pocket watch in the top drawer of the nightstand, so that I could take it out any time I needed to and think of him. The wound of his absence was still fresh. My girls didn't know it, but I still cried at night missing him.

The girls suggested taking a walk around the facility to get out of the room for a while once we were unpacked, but I wanted to meet and say hello to my roommate first. I pulled the first curtain back that led to the bathroom, and then did a half-knock on the side of the wall, before pulling the curtain back to Anna's room.

"Hello?" I called out.

"Hello?" she sounded startled.

"I'm sorry, I didn't mean to disturb or frighten you. My name is Judith. I'm your new roommate. I just wanted to say hello and introduce myself."

"Oh hello," she said with a relieved smile. "You must not be in a hurry."

"In a hurry?"

"To get to the bathroom," she replied. "Most of us are in a hurry."

"Oh, I don't have to go to the bathroom. I just came over to say hello," I said.

"You mean you came over without an aide?" she asked.

"It's only a couple feet," I laughed.

"You're a rebel," Anna laughed with me. "I like you already."

After introducing Carolyn and Cindy to Anna, my daughters suggested we continue our walk around the facility to get out of the room for a while. I thought that was a great idea, as I wanted to learn the layout of Pine Meadows so that I could take frequent walks throughout the day to get exercise, especially to visit the therapy gym.

As we were walking down the hallway, I noticed several of the residents who had their doors open were looking at us rather strangely. I didn't give it much of a thought though, as I was the new girl and it would take a while until I got to know everyone. We made our way past the nurses' station, which was a flurry of activity at that time of day, so no one raised their head to say hello. We turned to the left toward the activity room and library when we bumped into Kristi coming out of a resident's room.

"Hi Kristi!" I said with a smile.

She returned my smile with a frown, "What in the world are you doing out here by yourself? Did you press your call button?"

"I'm with my daughters," I replied, "And like I told you before, I'm perfectly capable of walking."

"In this facility, you must be accompanied by a nursing assistant at all times when you are up. Your family cannot assist you, it's a liability. That's just the rules here. Where were you headed?" she asked with a sigh. "I'll walk you the rest of the way."

"We were just out walking for exercise," Carolyn said. "We'll just go back to her room. We didn't realize the policy was so strict. We're sorry about the miscommunication."

"I'll walk with you," Kristi said.

I was embarrassed and ashamed. I've never been treated more like a child in all of my adult years. It took some time for the lump in my throat to subside and the tears in my eyes to clear. Not only did this place look like a jail, but it was beginning to feel like one too. I couldn't wait to do my time and get out. I was determined to work as hard as possible to get back home.

On the way back to the room, after I had settled down a bit, I asked Kristi, "Will I still be able to take walks in the hallways for exercise if I use my call button to have a nursing assistant walk with me?"

"Oh, we'd be happy to do that as long as we have time," she said. "But I can tell you, they probably have more time for that on second shift versus on first shift. Your best bet is to ask sometime around seven in the evening."

"What about walking to and from the dining room for meals? I don't want to eat in my room," I said.

"Again, we'll certainly do the best we can, but that's why every room has a wheelchair. If we're running short staffed or short on time, sometimes we have to use the wheelchairs to take residents to the dining room. I know it's not ideal, but you don't want to miss your meal," Kristi replied.

I glanced over at Carolyn and Cindy. I was quite livid. None of this was brought up in the initial tour with Joanna. I wanted to know what my daughters were thinking. *Was Carolyn still thinking that this nursing home was the highest rated in the area? Were they both still thinking that this was a satisfactory place for me to live?* I was about ready to ask what kind of restraints the staff used on us at night, only I was afraid to know the answer.

When we arrived back at the room, Kristi asked if I wanted to sit in the chair or get in bed. I told her I'd rather sit in the chair. She assisted me to the chair, handed me my call button, and reinforced that I should utilize it if I needed or wanted to get up for any reason and then wait until a nursing assistant or nurse arrived to help.

The girls both sat at the edge of the bed.

"We're sorry, Mom," Cindy said, "If we had known we were going to get you in trouble, we certainly wouldn't have suggested that walk."

"Don't worry about it," I said, fighting back tears again, "Like Kristi said, the assistants will walk with me when they can."

"That's the best way to look at it, Mother," Carolyn said, "We have to look at the positives here. You're going to be well taken care of. They only want what's best for you and they're looking out for your well-being."

I didn't reply. I just looked down at my lap. I just wanted to do my time and get out of this place. I promised them I would give Pine Meadows a fair chance and that I would do my part to work hard, I wasn't going to make a fuss.

It was almost dinnertime, so Carolyn and Cindy said their goodbyes and left, promising to return tomorrow to see how things were going.

After they left, I had to go to the bathroom before dinner, so I pressed my call button. It was twenty minutes before someone came to the door to assist me into the bathroom and another fifteen minutes until someone came to assist me out of the bathroom. By then, it was time to go to dinner. I asked to walk, but the nursing assistant said there was no time. I would have to ride in the wheelchair.

Chapter 5

When I arrived at the dining hall, the aide that brought me down asked me where I would like to sit. Since I'd never been there before, I really had no idea. I looked around the hall for an empty space and spotted Anna at a table with a couple of other women. She smiled warmly and waved me over.

"Over there," I pointed in Anna's direction.

Once settled, I said to Anna, "Thank you. I was starting to feel like the new girl in school again, not quite sure where I was going to sit."

"No problem," she said. "This is Ila," she pointed toward a tall woman with short dark brown hair and stylish dress. "And this is Denise," she gestured toward a shorter plump woman with graying hair wearing a sweatshirt that had been cross-stitched I Love My Grandchildren with all of the names of her grandchildren on it.

All three of the women were sitting in wheelchairs. I looked around the dining hall. Every resident was sitting in a wheelchair. I just shook my head. I knew some of them had to be able to walk also.

"What's wrong, Judith?" asked Ila.

"I came here to get stronger," I said. "I plan for this stay to be temporary. Once I am stronger and more independent, I want to return home. I promised my daughters I would work hard here to make that happen, but they won't let us do anything here."

"Oh Judith," Anna put her arm on my shoulder. "We all want to go home, but I've been here for five years, Ila's been here three, and Denise has been here six. We all felt the same way you did when we first arrived. I'm not saying that it's impossible, but please don't get your hopes up."

My heart sank a bit. These ladies appeared to be genuine, as Ila gave me a sympathetic smile. I wanted to tell them that I wasn't like them, that today was my first day here and that I was going to start therapy tomorrow. I didn't want to hurt their feelings, so I decided to let the topic of conversation drop.

During dinner, I learned that Anna used to be a home economics teacher at one of the local high schools. She was still married, but since her recent stroke and cancer diagnosis, which she had beaten and was in remission, her husband was unable to care for her at home since his own health was failing. She said he came to visit her as often as he could, which was usually in the mornings and early afternoons. She told me his name was Bob.

Ila told me that she was a housewife most of her life, and now she was widowed. Like me, she had come to Pine Meadows per the recommendation of her children after she had experienced a fall and broken her hip. Her hip had long since healed, yet she was still at Pine Meadows. She told me that her house had been sold at auction without her knowledge. And she, like me, had made her son her healthcare power of attorney, so she didn't have much choice in the matter.

Finally, Denise shared her story. She, like Ila and I, was also widowed. Denise had come to Pine Meadows after her family decided she could no longer manage her type-two diabetes properly at home. Denise claimed she was managing just fine, better, in fact, than the staff at Pine Meadows was doing. Denise said the worst part about being at Pine Meadows is that she missed her family. She said they don't come visit as often as she would like and she missed her grandchildren like crazy. "They're growing up so fast, and I'm missing every minute of it," she said with a tear in her eye.

After dinner was over, we all had to wait in our wheelchairs for a staff member to take us back to our rooms. Since there were so many residents and so few staff members, it took quite a while. I couldn't help but think that I would be back in my room already if I could have just walked on my own. I sighed. I was going to have to work on my patience if I was going to be spending any time at Pine Meadows.

That night was a difficult one. Although it was comforting to know that Anna, my new friend, was across the curtain, I still felt lonely. I felt like a prisoner in my bed, knowing that I couldn't get up without calling for someone to help me. I decided to turn the television on for a distraction. I kept the volume low, so as not to disturb Anna.

The television didn't help. This was not my home. This was not my bed. I missed Larry. Despite our age, we had still slept side by side every night. I missed the comfort of his touch. I flipped the switch on the lamp on my bedside table and looked at the family photos on the wall. How different those times were, we were all so happy. Larry was smiling in every photo. He was always smiling.

It was so unfair that he left me. How dare he leave me like this? He went and died and now I was stuck in this—this place. That was all well and good. He was having a grand old time up there in Heaven, while I was stuck in Pine Meadows with a call button.

No, no, I wasn't going to blame him. I knew in my heart that was wrong. It wasn't Larry's fault he died. We thought he was in good health. No one expected him to have a heart attack. I just missed him so much. I missed him so much that I physically felt pain. I shut the television off and just let the tears flow.

Chapter 6

The next day, I resigned myself to be in a better mood. It was therapy day. I was actually excited. I couldn't wait to do some exercise. One of the aides wheeled me down to the therapy gym at ten o'clock for my appointment and I met with one of the therapists, Jill. Jill explained that she would be doing my physical therapy evaluation and then Rob, her assistant, would be going through some exercises with me.

Jill's evaluation consisted of some strength testing, balance testing, and an analysis of how I walked. I hadn't walked in a couple of days other than the few feet from my bed to the bathroom with the assistance of an aide, so I was a bit wobbly. Jill suggested I try a walker with wheels.

"Oh no, I don't need one of those," I laughed.

"Your gait is a little unsteady," she said.

"My what?"

"Your gait. It's a fancy term for how you walk," she explained.

"That's only because I haven't walked in a day or so," I said.

"It's important that you walk every day Judith, to keep up your strength, or you will lose it," Jill said.

I wanted to scream – *They don't let us here!*

"I understand, I'm hoping this therapy will help with that," I said.

"For now, I'd really like you to try the walker and see what a difference it makes. You'll find that your balance is a lot more stable with the walker."

"Okay fine, I'll try it," I said, as I hung my head.

"Great!" she said, as if she was getting paid extra have try out a stupid walker.

So, I took a walk in the hallway with Jill and the wheeled walker. As she had assured me, my balance didn't falter a bit.

"Do you notice the difference?" she asked.

I did notice the difference, but I didn't want to admit it to her. It was only because I hadn't been allowed to walk that my legs had stiffened up. I was perfectly capable of walking without a walker. Walkers were for people with injuries or old people. I was only seventy-eight. Why wasn't she having me try a cane?

"Yes," I admitted, without making eye contact with her.

"I'd like to have you start using this walker for now and, as we go about your therapy, maybe we can progress you back off of it," she said.

"Okay," I said, resigned. I was learning that it wasn't worth trying to put up much of a fight about things here at Pine Meadows.

After the walker assignment, it was time for me to exercise with Rob. I was really looking forward to this portion of my therapy. Rob was fun and had me do several exercises to strengthen my legs, as well as my abdominal muscles, as he said those were imperative to balance. Rob informed me that some days he would be my therapist and some days he would not, but that everyone would be following the same treatment plan and the goals that had been written by Jill.

"What goals?" I asked.

"The goals for your therapy," Rob replied.

"Shouldn't I have written the goals?" I asked.

Rob looked sheepish. "Maybe talk to Jill about that?"

I felt bad putting Rob on the spot, because he was such a nice guy. That's when I noticed a makeshift set of stairs in the corner of the therapy gym.

"Rob, can you tell me if one of my goals is to be able to walk up and down those stairs over there? I'd really like to be able to walk up and down stairs again."

Rob opened his laptop and clicked a few buttons.

"Yes, it looks like Jill wrote a goal for you to be able to walk up and down the stairs with distant supervision, which means someone watching from a distance."

I smiled. At least one thing had gone my way.

At two o'clock, it was time for activities. The marker-board at the nurses' station said that today's activity was balloon volleyball. I wasn't particularly interested in balloon volleyball, but I was bored and figured it would be another opportunity to get some exercise. I pressed my call button a half hour early to ensure I would get there on time. This time, a nursing assistant showed up right away. Kelly offered to walk me down to the activity room if I would like.

"That would be great," I said.

As Kelly assisted me to stand up and head out the door, I started to take a couple of steps, before she stopped me, "Wait!"

I stopped, startled, not sure what had happened.

Kelly pulled out the wheeled walker from beside my closet and placed it in front of me. "Now we're ready," she said.

I wanted to literally thump my head. I forgot about the walker. What would my new friends think, seeing me walk into activities with a walker? Frail, old lady, that's what they would think. But I'd already committed to walking, and I wanted to get rid of this thing, so Kelly and I walked down to the activities room with my new walker.

"Nice ride!" Anna exclaimed as soon as she saw me walk into the room. She, Ila, and Denise had saved a seat for me. I had to smile. I knew she was trying to make me feel better. After all, Anna was bound to a wheelchair, and Ila and Denise both used walkers, although they were both in wheelchairs for the activity session.

"Did you get that at therapy today?" Ila asked.

"Yes," I said. "The therapist said I was a little wobbly."

"Which therapist did you have?" Denise asked.

I wracked my brain, but I just couldn't remember their names. That was weird. I had just seen them a few hours ago. I could remember what they looked like, but couldn't remember their names. How odd.

"You know, I can't remember off hand," I said. And that was going to bother me.

"It's okay, it doesn't matter," Anna said. "Let's play."

Chapter 7

The next morning, before breakfast, I had to go to the bathroom. I pressed my call button and waited for someone to arrive to assist me into the bathroom. After thirty minutes, no one arrived. I was beginning to think I was going to have an accident, so I pressed my call button again, wondering if maybe I didn't press it hard enough the first time. I waited another fifteen minutes, and then decided that I couldn't wait any longer. I got up by myself, without my walker, and headed into the bathroom. I made it there safe and sound.

I had only been in the bathroom for a couple of seconds when a nursing assistant knocked on the bathroom door.

"How did you get in here?" she asked.

"I walked," I replied.

"But did someone help you? Your call light is still on."

"I waited for almost an hour. I couldn't wait any longer," I said.

"You always have to have someone with you," she said in an exasperated tone. "And, you didn't even use your walker."

I was embarrassed that we were even having this conversation while I was on the pot.

"I made it here safely," I defended myself.

"I'm going to have to report this incident," the aide said. "We're probably going to have to use alarms on you."

After breakfast, I came back to my room to find someone had placed two small plastic pads in my room: one lying on my bed and one on my recliner chair. I asked the aide what they were and he explained to me that they were called motion alarms. He said that they would make a soft beep once I settled myself either in the recliner chair or the bed, but if I tried to get up from either place, a shrill alarm would go off to alert staff that I was up on my own. He said that if I used my call button for assistance, staff could to shut the alarms off before I got up.

I slumped my shoulders and hung my head. I had never felt more demeaned in my entire life. I had never heard of such a thing, putting an alarm on a human being. I felt like an animal at the zoo that wasn't allowed to leave certain parts of her cage. After my aide left, I picked up the telephone and called Carolyn.

"They just want to make sure you're safe, Mother," she said, after I explained the situation to her.

"You have no idea how ashamed I feel. I've lost all of my dignity here!"

"I'm sure it's only temporary Mom. Once they see that you are faithful about using your call light, they'll get rid of those alarms," she said.

I wished I had called Cindy.

Later that day, at lunch, I told my friends about my predicament. They were much more sympathetic than Carolyn.

"You poor thing," Denise said. "You've only been here two days and your experience has been just awful."

"Hopefully it's just temporary," Ila said.

"Hey, at least tomorrow we get to go to Wal-mart. That ought to cheer you up a bit," Anna chimed in.

I had completely forgotten about the Wal-mart trip. There had been a sign-up sheet in the activities room yesterday during balloon volleyball for anyone who wanted to go and the four of us had all signed up. I didn't really need anything; I just wanted to get out of Pine Meadows for a while.

The next morning at breakfast it was all we talked about. Ila talked about how she wanted to buy some new body wash and shampoo, Anna wanted to shop for some adult coloring books, and Denise wanted to buy some gifts for her grandchildren for the next time they came to visit. I decided I would shop for a new pair of shoes, ones that would help with my balance and be good for therapy.

At ten o'clock that morning, an aide arrived at my room, "Are you ready, Judith?"

"For what?" I asked.

"To go to Wal-mart," she replied.

"Oh yes! Yes."

When we returned from Wal-mart, I was flat-out exhausted. The activities department had arranged to have one staff member per resident on the trip, so each of us had someone with us at all times. I was allowed to walk with my walker throughout the store. It was the farthest I had walked in days. My body was really feeling the effects. I did, however, find a new pair of tennis shoes, and I was hoping these shoes would make a big difference at my next therapy session.

Yet, when the bus pulled into the drive, I was dreading the walk back to my room. My feet ached and my muscles were sore. As I stepped onto the platform to lower down from the bus to the ground with my assistant, I lost my footing, and tripped over my walker, falling to the ground.

Everyone gasped and a few yelped out loud, as my assistant did the best he could to grab hold of me, but it was too late. I hit the pavement headfirst. I was surprisingly conscious after the fall and able to tell that I hadn't broken any bones that I was aware of.

"I'm okay!" I announced immediately, despite my bruised pride.

"No, you're not," my assistant stated. "We need to get you checked out."

That's when I felt my face. I brought my hand down and realized it was covered in blood. I must have bashed myself up pretty good.

"Stay right there," he said, as he went inside to call for help.

The next thing I knew, a nurse was outside bandaging my face, and checking me over to make sure that I hadn't sprained or broken anything. She said she'd be calling the doctor, who would be in to see me later that day.

"Was she wearing a gait belt?" the nurse asked my assistant.

"No," he said, without making eye contact with her.

"She must wear a gait belt at all times from here on out. Please make a note of that in her chart."

"What's a gait belt?" I asked.

"Have you seen some of the residents wearing them?" my assistant asked. "A gait belt is a special belt that goes around your waist that you wear at all times when you're up that we use to help keep your balance should you start to have a fall."

I had seen some of the residents wearing those belts, and to be honest, they looked ridiculous in my opinion.

"This was just a fluke accident," I said. "I don't need one of those."

"It's our policy here that any time someone has a fall, he or she is required to wear a gait belt," the nurse said.

I sighed. I couldn't wait to be free of policies and rules.

Later that evening, in my room, the telephone rang. It was Carolyn. She said she was calling because the staff at Pine Meadows had called her to report that I had experienced a fall and that, while I was okay, I was going to be monitored a little more closely for a while to ensure my safety.

"I'm really worried about you Mom," Carolyn said. "But I'm glad they're going to be keeping a closer eye on you."

"No one said anything to me about keeping a closer eye on me. They just put this stupid belt on me that I have to wear at all times when I get up."

"It's just for your safety. They just want what's best for you. None of us want to see you fall and break a hip."

"I'm not going to fall and break a hip, Carolyn," I said.

"Things happen," she responded.

"I just can't wait to come back home," I said.

That's when she changed the subject.

The next morning was another therapy day. I was ready to get back at it, especially with my new shoes. I was surprised when I arrived at the therapy gym to find that Jill was going to be my therapist again. She had explained on the first day that she wouldn't see me again for another ten visits or so.

"I'm seeing you again so soon because you experienced a fall the other day," she explained. "I have to re-evaluate you."

"What does that mean?" I was almost scared to ask.

"It means that we might have to re-adjust your treatment plan a little bit. We'll see. We're going to do a lot of what we did the first day and go from there."

So, she repeated the same balance tests and strength tests and watched me walk with the walker again. She made some notes in her computer and then passed me over to Rob.

Rob again was his usual fun-loving self, however, this time he had me sit down and do some basic kicks and marches with my legs, much easier than what I had done the session prior. He didn't have me get on the mat table at all to do any abdominal exercises or core strengthening, as he called it. In fact, at the end of the session, he had me pedal a bike called a NuStep and said he was going to start it on the lowest resistance.

"Are we going to tackle the stairs today?" I asked Rob.

"I'm afraid that's not one of your goals this time around, Judith," Rob stated.

"What? The stairs have to be a goal. I need to be able to do them in order to go home."

"It looks like Jill really scaled down your treatment plan since your fall," he said. "I think she's afraid we were a bit too aggressive to start with."

"I have to be able to do those steps," I repeated.

"It's not one of your goals. I can't practice it with you, I'm sorry. It's the rules," Rob said.

Chapter 8

The following day was a Saturday, and Carolyn and Cindy dropped by for a visit. Neither of them had been there since the day I had moved in, so it was nice to see them. However, neither of them brought the grandchildren.

"They're just not ready for that yet," Cindy said.

I assumed she meant seeing their grandmother with a walker, sitting on a plastic pad that beeps, with a clunky cloth belt around her waist, and a button on a cord she had to press if she wanted to move. I wasn't ready for any of that yet either.

"It's okay," I said. "I plan on being back home soon anyway."

"That's what we wanted to talk to you about today Mom," Carolyn said "It hasn't been going so great for you here this past week."

"You have no idea what it's like here Carolyn! With all their rules and policies, I can hardly live."

"It's not just that Mom," Cindy chimed in. "What about your fall? Your face looks atrocious. What if that had happened at home and you were by yourself? I can't even imagine how you would have handled it."

"I wouldn't have had that stupid walker to trip over in the first place," I said. "I wouldn't have been in a van with a moving platform for old people just to get to Wal-mart."

The girls gave each other a look, and right then I knew my point was going nowhere. I had a bad feeling in the pit of my stomach that the possibility of going home was fading.

"The truth is Mom, right now we think that if you go home, someone should stay with you twenty-four seven, just to be on the safe side," Carolyn said. "And between Cindy and I, we can't make that happen."

"We've looked into hiring help to come into the house, but no one can stay during the night," Cindy said. "And Carolyn and I can't stay every night even taking turns."

"I will be fine at night," I said.

"But we're worried about you based on how things have been going here," Cindy said.

"Just give me a chance to turn that all around, please?"

"Okay," Carolyn said. "Let's try a couple more weeks."

The following Monday we had another activity group session and this time it was a baking group. It was good to get together with Anna, Ila, and Denise again. I hadn't seen them, other than short hellos to Anna when going to the bathroom, since the week prior and kind of missed our chats. They were my only social outlet anymore.

"Oh my, you really did a number on yourself," Ila said, in reference to my face.

"You poor thing. You look like you got beat up," Denise said.

"It'll heal. It's just one of those things," I said, trying to blow it off. I wanted to change the subject.

"We were all pretty scared for you," Anna said. "We're glad you're okay. Sorry you have to wear that stupid belt though."

"What belt?" I asked.

"The gait belt," Anna replied. "The one they make you wear when you're up."

"Oh yeah, this ridiculous thing," I said. "I hate this thing."

I told them about Carolyn and Cindy's visit and how they were worried about how things were going for me the past week at Pine Meadows. I explained the situation about the possibility of going home, but that there was no one who could stay with me at night.

"So, I guess I'm stuck here until I can prove that I can take care of myself either around the clock or at least throughout the night," I said. "Carolyn said we'd give it another couple of weeks."

"You're lucky your daughters are so involved in your care," Ila said.

And when she said that, I realized that I was. Poor Ila's family didn't pay much attention to her or visit her very often. Neither did Denise's grandchildren. I realized I shouldn't have been complaining as much as I had been around these women. I was pretty grateful for my daughters.

"What are we baking today?" I asked, changing the subject.

"We are baking peanut butter cookies," the activities director said.

"Who are we baking them for this time?" Anna asked.

Apparently, we baked for different people each time.

"We're baking these for the environmental services staff," she said.

With that, for the first time since I arrived at Pine Meadows, I felt good. I felt like I was a part of something positive. I had always enjoyed doing good things for other people. At least I knew I could look forward to baking group days at Pine Meadows.

"Are you coming to the meeting this afternoon?" Denise asked the next morning at breakfast.

"What meeting?" I asked.

"She's talking about the Resident Council meeting," Anna said. "I'm the president. We have a meeting this afternoon at two o'clock. Usually the meetings are closed, except to members of the council, but this one is open to anyone who would like to come."

"What do you talk about at a Resident Council meeting?" I asked.

"We talk about all kinds of things, like our care, how we're treated, suggestions to make things better, even the food!" she looked down at her plate and laughed. "The director of nursing, Nancy, and the nursing home administrator, Joanna, both come to the meetings to listen to our concerns and take notes."

"I'm coming, too," Ila said. "I have a concern about Jackie," she said in a quieter tone. "She's been using some colorful language when she answers my light."

"I want to talk about my insulin monitoring," Denise said. "They try to limit my intake and then wonder why my sugar goes so low. Then, they end up giving me a sugary snack to make it go back up. All the while, I'm feeling sick. If I could just eat how I want to eat, I could have it much more controlled."

"Is there anything you want to talk about Judith?" Anna asked.

I thought it over. There were so many things, all of their rules and policies, that I didn't agree with. I felt like I had so many complaints, but I was scared to make a scene.

"I'll have to think about it. I'm not sure," I said.

For some reason, I was nervous when it came time for the meeting later that afternoon. I sat down with Ila and Denise. Anna, as the president, sat up front with Joanna and Nancy. I wasn't sure what to expect. I looked around and saw about thirty other residents had joined us for the meeting.

Folks brought up all kinds of issues, one at a time of course, by raising their hands. Anna, Joanna, and Nancy took notes as each resident brought up his or her concern. One resident mentioned that he had been timing how long it took for the aides to answer his call light. He said the average time was seventeen minutes and he felt that was unacceptable. Joanna assured him that they were working on increasing staffing, as she had assured my family and I before my admission, to ensure that wait time would soon be decreased.

Another resident brought up the fact that the water in the shower room was cold (and she was right), another made a complaint that there weren't enough food choices on the menu at meal times, an additional resident stated that he didn't like using the mechanical lift to get in and out of his chair and didn't know why he couldn't get back into therapy to try to get stronger so he could get up without the lift.

Ila brought up her concern about the nursing assistant, Jackie, using swear words and unsuitable language while helping her throughout the day. Ila stated that she wasn't one who was easily offended, but said that Jackie often used the F word. Ila said that she didn't want to get anyone in trouble, but that she was offended by the use of this word.

After Ila spoke, I noticed Joanna and Nancy give each other a look and then proceed to make notes in their respective notebooks. Jackie had never been my aide before, but like Ila, I wouldn't want to be treated that way. However, I had a bad feeling that Jackie was about to get reprimanded, and that might not turn out well for Ila if Jackie was her regular aide.

Finally, it was Denise's turn to bring up her concerns about her diabetes and insulin monitoring. As soon as she began to speak, Nancy interrupted her.

"Denise, you bring this up at every resident council meeting. We've talked about this before," Nancy said.

"But I feel I have a valid concern," Denise said.

"Your nurse has explained to you time and again why we have to monitor your intake the way that we do and why we have to check your sugar at specific times of day. If your sugar goes low, which happens to every diabetic from time to time, we do have to be sure that we have snacks on hand to bring it back up," Nancy explained. "It's all a part of having type-two diabetes, which, unfortunately, is the condition that you have."

"If I could just monitor my own intake—"

"Denise, it's our job to ensure that we protect your health. If we were to let you monitor your own intake, we would have no idea how many carbs you were ingesting, and therefore, no idea what dose of your diabetes medicine to administer or how much insulin to give you in an emergency."

Denise just hung her head. I could tell she'd been defeated on this issue multiple times in the past. My heart went out to her.

Anna asked if anyone else had any concerns they'd like to share before the meeting adjourned. I debated whether or not to bring up my many concerns regarding my opinion of the unfairness of the rules and policies I'd been subjected to since my arrival at Pine Meadows. But I was afraid that, like Denise, I would just get rejected. And I didn't want to make a spectacle of myself right before I was supposed to be going back home. So, I kept my mouth shut. And Anna adjourned the meeting.

Chapter 9

The next morning felt like a circus at Pine Meadows. There was a hub of activity in the hallway and it seemed like staff was fluttering around like birds at a feeder. The nursing assistants were surprisingly running like mad to answer call lights in a timely manner. I noticed I only had to wait a couple of minutes until Kristi came to assist me into the bathroom. She then waited for me to finish, instead of leaving like she usually did, and walked me down to breakfast, instead of wheeling me in the wheelchair.

When I arrived at the dining hall for breakfast, I noticed that most of the residents who were ambulatory had been walked down for their meal, as I had, and every single resident was wearing a gait belt, like me. That was unusual. One of the nurses, Dawn, was coming around putting ID bands on all of us that stated our names and birthdates and any allergies we had.

When the gals arrived, I gave them the most puzzled look, "What is going on around here today?" I asked.

"State's here for an inspection," Anna said.

"What does that mean?"

"Every couple of years, this particular agency has to come in and inspect all nursing homes to make sure they're following all of the proper guidelines. Unfortunately, some nursing homes get lax after a while and start to let some of the rules slide. These agencies come in for our, the residents', safety to make sure that the staff is following all of the proper guidelines."

"Well Pine Meadows should pass with flying colors when it comes to following the rules," I said.

"You'd be surprised," Anna said. "That's why we have the resident council meetings."

"The what?" I asked.

"The resident council meetings," she said. "The one you came to yesterday."

I didn't know what she was talking about, but I decided to let it slide.

"Things are great when the state is here," Denise said. "They have to follow the Resident Right's law, which means I get to eat whatever I want, whenever I want."

"And the aides are on their best behavior," Ila said.

"Does this mean it wasn't a fluke that Kristi answered my call light so fast this morning?" I asked.

"Nope," said Ila. "They're going to be on the call lights like hot potatoes for the next three days. Enjoy it while it lasts."

So, for breakfast, Denise ordered pancakes and sausage, and after it was over, none of us had to wait to return to our rooms. Kristi ensured I was comfortable before she left and that I had everything I needed.

The next thing I knew, Joanna and a young man dressed in a suit and tie arrived at my door. The young man introduced himself as Jeff. Jeff said he was from the state organization and was hoping to ask me a few questions about my stay at Pine Meadows if that was okay. I told him of course.

"Those are some pretty significant bruises you have on your face there, Ms. March. How did those happen?" Jeff asked.

"Oh! I'm so embarrassed," I said. "I was getting out of the van after we took a trip to Wal-mart and I tripped over my walker on the platform and fell head first onto the ground."

"Was anyone with you?" he asked.

I was trying hard to remember. This was a few days ago. "Yes, I believe so. Yes, there was. There was a male assistant with me. I can't remember his name."

"Were you wearing a gait belt?" Jeff asked.

This I could remember, because I remember them making me wear one after the fact. "No, I wasn't," I said.

I noticed Joanna hang her head as I answered this question.

"I see you have one in your room now," Jeff said.

"Yes, they have me wear one now every time I get up," I said.

"I see you have motion alarms here in your room as well. Tell me the story behind those. Why do you have those?"

"Well, they told me to always use my call button and wait for assistance prior to getting up. No matter what. But one day I had to go to the bathroom and it was quite an emergency. I had pressed my call button, but I had waited over a half hour and no one came. At that point, I took it upon myself to take myself to the bathroom. It was either that or wet myself," I said.

I noticed Joanna's face turning a bright shade of red.

"Once I had situated myself in the bathroom, an assistant did arrive and found that I had taken myself. She reported me for violating the rules and they put these alarms on me," I continued.

"I see," said Jeff. He turned to Joanna, "I'm not sure if you're aware, but new studies have shown that alarms such as these are not as effective in preventing falls as proper staffing. If you have the proper amount of staff per resident to be able to answer call lights in a timely manner, you could prevent falls at a much more optimal rate than utilizing these motion alarms."

"Thank you for that information," Joanna said. "I do appreciate that. And we are currently hiring, so hopefully we will be able to meet those staffing requirements very soon."

"One more question, how do you feel about your stay here at Pine Meadows so far overall?" Jeff asked.

Joanna looked at me with big eyes. I could tell she was pleading with me that this was not the time to air out multiple complaints.

"While Pine Meadows has a lot of rules and policies, the staff here has all been very nice to me. I haven't been here too long, and I am hoping in another couple of weeks, after some intense therapy here, I can return to my own home. So, I see this as a temporary place for me."

"Sure, of course," Jeff said. "Thank you for your time, Judith."

The next couple of days were like a welcome break from the usual. Our call lights were answered promptly, we were all treated respectfully, and my motion alarms were even removed. It was like a dream come true. I couldn't wait for my next therapy session to see what would change there.

Rob greeted me when I arrived, having walked down with the assistance of my aide. He had me start off on the NuStep bike for ten minutes. I asked him if we could please increase the intensity today and, to my delight, he said yes. He increased me to level three and I could actually feel something working in my arms and legs.

After completing the NuStep, Rob had me lie down on the mat table to do some lying-down exercises. I wasn't overly thrilled at first, as the exercises were entirely too easy. Rob had me do some ankle pumps, leg lifts, kicks to the side, knee bends, bridging, and hip squeezes. When we were done, I couldn't help but express my frustration.

"Rob, I hate to say it, but these exercises are just too easy for me."

"I know," he said quietly. "But I have to follow Jill's treatment plan. Let's try to look at it in another way. These exercises might be too easy for you to do just three times per week in therapy, but you can also do them in your room every day. You can do them in the mornings and in the evenings to help build your strength. I can even print you a handout, so you don't forget what exercises we've done. Would that help?"

"Oh Rob, that would be wonderful," I said.

He printed me off a handout and I walked back to my room with an assistant. I put the handout on my nightstand where I could easily access it. It seemed like things were finally starting to go my way and maybe I'd be heading home before I knew it.

Chapter 10

Carolyn and Cindy came for another visit the following Saturday. They noticed right away that my motion alarms were gone and Cindy mentioned that my face was looking better.

"Thank you," I said. "I think so too."

"What's this?" Carolyn asked, looking at the sheet of paper on my nightstand.

I explained to her that I had been going to therapy, as promised, and that I had been doing my exercises with my therapist. I told her that he gave me a copy of the exercises to do in my room on my own so that I could work on getting stronger, even when I wasn't in therapy.

"That's a good idea," Cindy said.

"Is it helping?" Carolyn asked.

"I just started," I replied. "But yes, I think so."

"Listen, Mom, I really hope that it is, because we'd like to take you home for the day tomorrow to go through some things at the house. Yes, there's still the possibility of you returning home, but we really need to downsize regardless. Joanna says you can come home with us for the day as long as we check you out at the nurses' station and then sign you back in when we return. Does that sound okay?"

It sounded wonderful to me. I hadn't been home in weeks, even if just for the day. I couldn't wait to be around the things that reminded me of Larry and just to be in my own environment again, without rules and policies to follow. I wasn't looking forward to getting rid of anything in the house, but just to be home again, I was thankful.

"That sounds great," I said.

The next morning, at nine o'clock sharp, the girls arrived to check me out and drive me back home. We had to take my walker and I had to wear my gait belt, of course, but I planned on ditching those things as soon as we got to the house.

When we arrived, I felt an overwhelming sense of relief. I imagined myself there to stay. I wondered if my girls realized how difficult it was going to be to get me to go back to Pine Meadows. The house smelled just as it had when I left it, still with a hint of Larry's cologne.

We walked into the living room, and it was full of boxes, clothes, and other items from upstairs. It looked like the girls had pretty much brought down everything from Larry's and my bedroom, as well as plenty of things from the four guest bedrooms for me to sort through. It was going to take more than a day to sort and I let them know that.

"This is going to take much longer than a few hours to finish," I said.

"I realize that Mom, but we have to get a head start on it now," Carolyn said. "A lot of things, especially Dad's clothes, have to get taken somewhere, like to Goodwill or a place like that."

I looked over at the pile that included his clothes. I didn't want to get rid of them, not yet anyway. I knew they weren't going to bring him back, but something about having his clothes was comforting, and I didn't want some stranger wearing them.

"Where do you want me to take them?" Cindy asked, interrupting my thoughts.

"What?" I asked.

"Where do you want me to take Dad's clothes? Goodwill? Or to the church donation box?" she asked again.

"The church," I said, feeling sorrowful.

As the day went on, we also went through a lot of my old clothes, things I didn't wear anymore, to send to the church, as well as some old costume jewelry, several pairs of shoes, and multiple jackets and winter coats I no longer needed or wore. We also sorted through old boxes of receipts that were more than seven years old and threw those away. Plus, Cindy convinced me to part with my old doll collection and donate it to Goodwill, after more than forty years of collecting.

Carolyn announced that she had figured out Larry's bookkeeping program on the computer for keeping track of the finances for the household. She said that she had been able to keep everything going so far, but that the cost of me staying at Pine Meadows was adding up. She said we would have to make a decision soon whether or not I would be coming home or staying at Pine Meadows permanently and selling the house.

"There is no reason I can't come home right now," I said.

"Can you climb the stairs?" Cindy asked.

"Not yet, but I could continue to sleep on the sofa and I could sponge bathe in the half bath downstairs. Ila told me that there are home health care workers to come to the house who could work with me on getting stronger and being able to eventually go up the stairs," I said.

"That's true," Carolyn said. "But, what does your therapist think?"

"My who?" I asked.

"Your therapist. The one who does exercises with you at Pine Meadows."

I was drawing a blank, so I decided to just answer nonchalantly, "Oh, who cares what she thinks?"

"It's pretty important what she thinks Mom," Cindy said. "The therapist is usually the one who recommends if you're physically strong enough to make it at home."

I resolved to pay more attention when I returned to Pine Meadows.

"I know I can get around the house without this walker," I said.

I set the walker off to the side and proceeded out of the living room toward the dining room. As I made my way through the dining room, I found myself grasping for furniture in order to keep my balance. I never had to do that before. I guess it didn't really matter too much, that's what the furniture was there for, and I was glad it was so close together. I walked in toward the kitchen and realized that the furniture wasn't quite as close together in my large kitchen as it had been in my living room and dining room. I tried to stay close to the wall, so I could use it for support, but it wasn't enough. I slid down the side of the wall like a limp noodle.

"Mom!" Cindy called out, as I made my way to the floor.

She and Carolyn rushed to my side, as I lay on the floor like a sack of potatoes.

"Are you okay, Mother? Are you hurt?" Carolyn asked.

"Just my pride," I said.

"I don't know how we're going to get you back up," Carolyn said. "We might have to call the rescue squad."

"Oh, heavens no," I replied. "I'll crawl over to that kitchen chair and the two of you can help me in it."

Despite my dignity, that's exactly what we did. I crawled across the kitchen on my hands and knees to the nearest kitchen chair and the girls helped me up into it.

"Obviously, you do need that walker," Carolyn said. "And how's a walker going to fit in this half bath?" She pointed in the direction of the half bathroom on the first level.

"It'll fit," I said, still blushing from my trip to the floor.

Carolyn promptly got out a tape measure. She brought my walker in from the living room and measured its width in front of me. She proceeded toward the half bathroom and measured the width of the doorway.

"It's not going to work Mom. The walker is wider than the doorway," she said.

"Then I'll just have to go in sideways," I said.

She rolled her eyes.

"Hey Mom, what's this?" Cindy asked, as she came into the kitchen holding a small lock box.

"I've never seen that before either," Carolyn said.

"Oh, it's— it's nothing," I said, recognizing immediately what it was.

"Well, is it something we should keep or is it something we should get rid of?" Carolyn asked.

"We should keep," I said, a little too quickly. And then, after a brief pause, I said, "In fact, I'd like to take that back to Pine Meadows with me. It's something that was important to your father and me."

"Okay, whatever you say," Carolyn said.

When we returned to Pine Meadows, it was almost with the same amount of dread as I felt on my first day. I didn't want to be back. My only saving grace was that this time I knew I had friends, Anna, Ila, and Denise, who were going to make this miserable experience just a little bit more manageable.

Carolyn checked me back in at the nurses' station and instead of just signing a paper that I had returned, she had to fill out an entire report of our outing, including any incidence of a fall. Of course, she had to check the Yes box, which meant she had to wait to speak with a nurse before leaving the facility. Carolyn had to stay and report to the nurse the exact nature of my fall, where it happened, how it happened, and what we had done about it. Here I was, getting another F on my report card at Pine Meadows.

Chapter 11

A couple of days later, the activities director decided to take a select few of us out to eat for lunch. The group included Anna, Ila, Denise, and I, along with about ten other residents. I was thankful all of my friends were coming along. We were going to one of the local steakhouses.

As we were making our way toward our table, I made sure to sit with the ladies, I couldn't help but just enjoy the fact that we were out of the facility for a bit. So many meals in the dining hall start to feel redundant after a while. I was thankful for our activities department for the work that they did and for making the effort to get us out of Pine Meadows for a short period of time.

After we had ordered, Denise thankful she could order whatever she wanted, Anna said that she had an announcement to make. She wasn't her usual jovial self this time.

"And I don't want anyone to be sad," she said. "But you all know I had that doctor's appointment yesterday…"

If I had known she had a doctor's appointment the day before, I had forgotten.

"Well, the doctor said my cancer is back," she said matter-of-factly.

"Oh Anna…" Denise said, as she put an arm around Anna's shoulders.

"I'm so sorry to hear that," I said.

"What can we do?" Denise asked.

"There's nothing you can do," Anna said. "Other than pray, I guess."

"Yes, we will pray," Ila said.

"But I'm going to fight," Anna said. "The doctor said the cancer is in my lung and in my lymph nodes this time, and that it's inoperable. But he also said I'm a candidate for both chemo and radiation, even at my age, so I'm going to fight this."

"We'll be with you every step of the way," Denise said.

"Even when I lose my hair?" Anna said with a smile.

I had to smile with her. She just gave off that vibe. I couldn't imagine being as strong as she was. She had already had cancer and beat it. She thought she had won. Now here she was, starting the fight back up again, this time older and maybe not as tough as she had been the first time around, but her spirit was still the same.

"Even when you lose your hair," Ila said, seriously. "Who's going to go with you to your appointments?"

"My children will try to go to as many as they can," Anna said. "But the ones that they can't, the staff at Pine Meadows will have to arrange for me to have a ride to and from. My husband's just not up for the trips."

I knew what Ila was thinking. Thank goodness Anna had a supportive family who was willing to go with her to and from appointments. And then I got to thinking, *My children are the same.* If I were in Anna's shoes, Carolyn and Cindy would do whatever they could to ensure that one or the other or both of them were along for every single one of my appointments. I may have been bitter that they put me in Pine Meadows, but I still had to be grateful for them.

Anna didn't want to spend the rest of lunch dwelling on her medical issues, so she changed the subject. We talked about everything from the staff at Pine Meadows to the food to the men. Ila thought Thomas was good looking, Denise thought Joe was a catch, and Anna thought all the men were worth a second glance, even though she was married. They asked me what my opinion was.

"Oh, it's too soon after Larry for me to pay much attention," I said.

"Come on," Anna said. "It doesn't hurt you to just look. No one says you have to marry the guy. Let's hear it. If you had to pick one guy at Pine Meadows just to play a game of Uno with, who would it be?"

I had to think long and hard. I hadn't given this much thought at all. But Anna was pressing for an answer.

"I guess Pat," I said.

"Good choice!" Denise said.

"He is really good looking," Ila pointed out.

"Pat is a fine choice," Anna said. "He's single. You two have a very similar story. His wife passed away several years ago, which is when he came to Pine Meadows. He wasn't a big fan of it either at first, but now I think he's getting used to it. You see him hanging out with that group of guys for coffee after breakfast. And in the summertime, he likes to sit outside on the front lawn and get some sun, which gives him a nice-looking tan."

"How do you know so much about him?" I asked.

"Anna knows everything about everyone," Denise said.

"It's true," Anna chuckled.

After we got back from lunch, Kristi came to my room to tell me it was time for another therapy session.

"I don't need therapy," I said. As sad as I was over Anna's diagnosis, I certainly wasn't in the mood for a counseling session.

"What are you talking about, Judith? You usually really enjoy therapy."

"I've never been to therapy before. Why would I start now?" I snapped back.

Kristi appeared confused at first, then it was almost as if a look of realization appeared over her face.

"Judith, this is physical therapy, exercises to help you get stronger so that hopefully you can go home someday."

I thought it over. She seemed genuine, like she wasn't trying to trick me.

"Okay, I'll go."

When we arrived at the therapy gym, everything looked familiar and I remembered being there before. I was grateful to Kristi for explaining things to me and felt a little guilty for snapping at her, but I didn't apologize. I wasn't really sure why.

My therapist was named Sammy this time. She told me that Jill heard that I had experienced another fall at home and was again worried that we might be overdoing it in therapy. She said that Jill wanted to stick to some pretty basic exercises, utilizing the NuStep and some seated leg exercises. I felt a bit defeated, but went along with what Sammy said. I asked Sammy if I could have a handout of the seated exercises to do in my room like Rob had given me of the lying-down exercises.

"Sure!" Sammy said. "We don't very often get people as motivated as you."

"I really want to go home," I said. "Do you think you could talk to Jill about my therapy? I think it's too easy. I know I've had a couple of falls, but I think it's because I'm not working hard enough. And I really want to be able to go up and down the stairs. I have stairs at home."

"I can try," Sammy said. "I'll do my best!"

I felt good after therapy. I felt like maybe I was finally getting somewhere. I was hopeful that I would be practicing the stairs during my next session and doing some higher-level activities to help with my balance. I would keep my fingers crossed.

Chapter 12

The following week in activities, as ironic as it was, we were scheduled to play cards. Not Uno but another game called Skip-Bo that required multiple people to play at one time. The activities director divided us up into groups of five to play the game and my group consisted of: Ila, Anna, Joe, me, and, of course, Pat. Anna had to wink at me several times as soon as the groups were divided up and she noticed Pat was in our group. I tried my best to avoid eye contact with her.

Anna was sure to arrange the seating so that I was sitting between her and Pat. Throughout the card game, though, I found myself getting more and more confused for some reason. Everyone else seemed to be getting the hang of it, but I was getting more and more lost. Anna, being the friend that she was, completely ignored the fact that I was having difficulty and let Pat be the one to help me. He was an absolute gentleman about it. He walked me through which card to play at what time and helped me reason out why to play each card, even if it meant beating him in that round!

I had to keep reminding myself that I had just lost Larry and that I wasn't looking to start a relationship with another man. But if I was, it certainly might have been Pat. He was kind, patient, and good-natured. He was even funny. He made several jokes at the table that everyone found humorous.

After we were done playing cards, he told me his story.

Pat told me that he and his wife, Betty, had been married forty-eight years when she passed away of pancreatic cancer three years ago. He said it was a short battle. Pat said before that, for the most part, Betty had always been his caregiver, taking care of all the meals, house cleaning, and bill paying. When she passed away, his one and only son felt that there was no way

Pat could make it on his own at home, so he decided Pat should live at Pine Meadows. Pat told me he fought tooth and nail to be able to stay at home and even tried to convince his son to hire private duty aides, but his son was unrelenting. Now his house had been sold and Pine Meadows was his forever home. He said he was slowly getting used to the idea, but it would never be the same.

I told him my story about Larry just recently passing away and the girls feeling the same about me—believing I couldn't make it on my own at home and feeling like I needed to live at Pine Meadows. I told him how I was hopeful, however, that I would be able to return home soon after a good bout of therapy and getting stronger.

"Your house isn't sold yet then?" he asked.

"No, not yet," I said. "But my daughters are eager to get rid of everything inside of it."

"That's too bad," he said.

"I'm hopeful they're just de-cluttering so that when I come home there will be less for me to fret over," I said.

"For your sake, I hope so too," he said. "Were you able to bring many of your important belongings with you to Pine Meadows?"

"Some, not all, but most of them," I said, thinking of the lock box.

"I was able to bring a few things of Betty's," he said. "A bottle of her perfume, a painting she painted, and a book of poems she wrote."

It made me feel better that he was still talking about his wife and speaking of her like he missed her. I still missed Larry a lot. I didn't want Pat to get the wrong idea. I could tell that he wasn't.

"Those are really nice items to hold onto," I said. "All I have of Larry's here so far is his pocket watch."

It was then that the aides came to wheel us back to our rooms.

"It was nice talking with you, Judith. I hope we can do it again sometime," Pat said.

"Likewise," I said.

At dinner that evening, Anna, Ila, and Denise had to know every detail of my date, as Anna called it, with Pat.

"Isn't he a perfect gentleman?" Anna asked. "He just swept you off your feet, didn't he?"

"Why? What did he do?" Denise asked.

"He's a nice guy," I said. "We are not a couple."

"Oh, he helped her play Skip-Bo – helped her win Skip-Bo, beating all of us," Anna laughed.

"And they were the last two at the table after we all left," Ila winked.

"We were just talking," I said. "He told me his story. I told him mine. He told me about his wife. He still misses her quite a bit, like I still miss my Larry. If anything, we bonded over that."

"Sounds like the budding of a nice friendship," Denise said.

"Thank you," I said.

That night, as I lay in bed, I wondered if I really had been unfaithful to Larry by talking to Pat. Larry was my one true love and that was never going to change. Pat was just an acquaintance, someone I had just met and started a conversation with. I wouldn't consider what we did to be flirting. But maybe it was. Maybe I shouldn't have let him help me with the card game. That was something Larry would have done for me if he were still here. He wouldn't have let another man do that.

But he wasn't still here. And if I was going to live at Pine Meadows for now, I was going to have to make friends, female and male. I decided that what I did wasn't wrong, and that I could continue to talk to Pat if I wanted to. He was still grieving his wife just like I was still grieving my husband, so he wasn't going to come on to me, I was sure of that. And we could build a friendship over our mutual grief.

I opened my nightstand drawer and took out Larry's pocket watch.

"You're always going to be the love of my life," I said, as tears formed in my eyes.

Chapter 13

The next day was hair day at Pine Meadows, which was a big day. A local salon owner came in and did hair for all of the residents who were willing to pay the fee for either just a cut, a cut and style, or a cut and perm. I hadn't had my hair done since before Larry passed away, so I was very much looking forward to this day. Carolyn had given me the money for the works, so I was planning on having the cut, perm, and style.

Ila always got her hair done on hair days. Anna was hit or miss, but planned to get her hair done this time. And Denise hardly ever got much more than a cut every now and then.

Hair appointments were after breakfast, so it was lunchtime until everyone got to see each other's new 'dos.

"Wow, look at you!" Anna said, when she saw me. "You look like a whole new woman."

"You do look great," Ila said.

"So do you both," I said.

"Can you tell I got mine cut?" Denise asked.

"Yes, it looks nice," I said, even though I couldn't tell.

I felt good. I was starting to feel like I truly belonged with this group of women. Not that I didn't want to return home. I knew once I got home, they wouldn't be there, but Anna, Ila, and Denise were starting to feel like my family in a way. I was sure going to miss them once I did go back home. I didn't have too many lady friends at home. Most of Larry's and my friends had been couple friends. It would be too awkward to spend time with them now, after his passing. Maybe I could come back and visit Anna, Ila, and Denise after I returned home. I was sure Carolyn and Cindy would give me a ride every now and then.

"Did you hear about the prom?" Denise asked, interrupting my thoughts.

"What prom?" I asked.

"Every year, the activities department puts on a prom for the residents," Anna explained. "It's a big deal. We all get dressed up and go down to the activities room and they treat it like a real high school prom. They play music from our era, you know, from when we were in high school. You're allowed to bring a date if you want, but you don't have to. Most of us just go for the fun of it."

"When is it?" I asked. I didn't have any fancy clothes with me and would have to ask Carolyn to bring in something from home.

"Next week," Ila said. "Tuesday afternoon."

"That sounds like a lot of fun," I said. "Are you all going?"

"Yes, of course," Anna said. "We wouldn't miss it for the world. It's one of the few things they do around here that's actually entertaining."

That evening, I spoke to Carolyn on the phone about the prom. I told her that I would need one of my evening gowns from the house and that I would need it by next week Tuesday.

"Just what exactly is this prom all about Mother?" she asked.

"It's just for fun Carolyn. They're taking us back to our high school days."

"Is there going to be dancing? How are you going to dance with your walker? I'm afraid you're going to have another fall."

"The activities staff will be there, Carolyn. And I doubt there's going to be any hardcore hip hop dancing as you young folks would say," I laughed. "Can you please just bring me my evening gown? I just want to look nice is all."

"I suppose so," she said.

But I could tell she still wasn't too keen on the idea when we hung up.

The following Tuesday came and my aide helped me get dressed up in my evening gown. Carolyn had been nice enough to even bring me some jewelry to match, so I felt I looked pretty good. My aide wheeled me down to the activities room in my wheelchair, but we took my walker along so that I could stand and dance with the assistance of one of the activities staff.

When we arrived, the activities room was already full. They had set up round tables with tablecloths with fancy plates and silverware for our meal. Someone had set up a disco ball over the dancing area, as well as streamers coming down from the ceiling. There wasn't a DJ, but one of the activities staff members was looking over an iPad that was connected to speakers, playing music from the 1950s and 1960s. I wasn't really sure why, but there was a stage set up with a microphone toward the front of the room. I wondered if we would have an emcee for the event.

I found the ladies sitting at a table not far from the stage and made my way toward them. They had, of course, saved a seat for me. They all looked stunning.

"You all look so beautiful," I said.

"You look great!" Denise said. "I love your jewelry. Did your daughter bring it?"

"Yes," I replied. "For some reason, she wasn't too thrilled about this prom, but she relented and brought me the dress and jewelry. Otherwise, I would have been in a world of hurt!" I laughed.

"I was lucky enough to have this here already," Ila said. "I'm not sure why I ever packed it to come here, wishful thinking I guess."

"We're going to have a great time today," Anna said with a smile, and for a moment, I forgot that her cancer had returned. She was always smiling, always ready for a good time. As the leader of our group, she had more pep than the rest of us combined. She told us that her husband was ill and couldn't make it, but that wasn't going to slow her down.

Before the dancing began, the food was served. It wasn't like our usual meal at Pine Meadows. This meal was special. We started off with a greens salad with honey mustard dressing, followed by twice baked potatoes, fried catfish, and then chocolate cheesecake truffles. I was stuffed at the end of the meal.

Once we were done with our feast, the music began playing a bit louder, meaning it was time to dance. Anna, of course, was the first one out on the dance floor in her wheelchair. As expected, multiple activities staff members were also on the dance floor to ensure the safety of all residents, but after Anna's initiative, other residents joined her, including me. It was a prom, after all, and we were there to have fun. After a while, Ila came over as well, and even Denise with her walker.

After several peppy songs, the staff played a couple of lower-key songs. Anna stayed on the floor and danced with a couple of gentlemen residents who twisted her in her chair, but Denise, Ila, and I went back to our seats. It wasn't long, however, until I felt a tap on my shoulder. It was Pat!

"Would you care to dance?" he asked.

"Sure," I said, my face blushing. I looked over and Ila and Denise, who both nodded.

As I walked out onto the dance floor with Pat, I realized it was going to be quite awkward to dance with a walker, but he didn't seem to mind it, nor did he seem to mind the staff member looming over us to ensure I didn't have another fall.

"You look nice," he said. "Not that you don't look nice every day. You look especially nice today."

"Thank you," I said. "My daughter brought this dress in from home. It's one of my favorites."

I didn't tell him about all the times I wore it out with Larry to dinner parties and events for his work.

"How have things been going for you lately?" Pat asked. "Any word on how soon you'll be able to go home?"

"Not yet. But my therapy is going good." In that moment, I drew a blank as far as what I had been working on in therapy, so I just let it go at that.

"What about you?" I asked. "How are things going for you?"

"Well, my son came to visit the other day. That was a nice surprise."

"Yeah, that is nice," I said.

"He said that my grandson is joining the Navy after graduation as a nuclear engineer," Pat said.

"Wow, you must be so proud of him!" I exclaimed.

"I am," Pat said. "But when I asked Dave if I would get to see him before he ships out, Dave said he's just too busy with graduation coming up and that he more than likely wouldn't be able to stop in."

"Oh, I'm so sorry Pat," I said.

Pat just frowned. I couldn't tell if he was fighting back tears, but I wouldn't blame him if he was.

After the dance, we went back to our respective tables. The staff played some more peppy music and we danced and laughed. Anna stayed on the dance floor pretty much the entire evening. At one point, Joe asked Denise to dance, which made Anna, Ila, and I all swoon. Pat and I danced to a few other slower songs together and had a nice time.

Toward the end of the evening, one of the staff members went up on the stage where the microphone was located. She announced that we were going to take a vote for Prom King and Prom Queen and that there were two voting boxes located in the back on the activities room. She said that we were to write the names of those we would like to vote for and slip them in the respective box and then the activities staff would tally up the votes and announce the winners as soon as everyone was done voting.

I immediately knew who I was voting for. I would be voting for Anna for Prom Queen and Darrel, the gentlemen she danced with most of the night, for Prom King. I hoped everyone else would too. That would make Anna so happy. I made my way to the back of the activities room and cast my ballot with ease. I could tell some of the others were really struggling with who to vote for and looking around the room with questioning looks as to who made the greatest impression that night.

After everyone cast their votes, the staff took the boxes out and counted the ballots outside of the room. One of the staff members came back in and whispered something in the ear of the staff member at the microphone. The staff member at the microphone stepped up to make her announcement.

"Ladies and gentlemen, we officially have a winner for Prom King and Prom Queen. Our Prom King this year is Pat DeWalter."

I was so happy for Pat! He deserved it. After telling me the story about his grandson, he deserved a bit of happiness, even if it was in the form of a paper sash and a makeshift crown. Pat walked up to the podium, his face blushing, but with a smile on his face. He sat in one of two chairs reserved for the Prom King and Queen.

"And our Prom Queen this year is … Judith March!"

Me? How could it be me? I was so sure that it would be Anna that I hadn't even dreamed it would be me. I almost couldn't stand up to go up front and receive my own paper sash. One of the activities staff members came over to assist me and together we walked up the ramp on to the stage. Pat was smiling even bigger now. The ladies put on my sash, my crown, and handed me a bouquet of flowers and had me sit down next to Pat for pictures. They said these pictures would be posted outside of the activities room on the bulletin board and also in the Pine Meadows newsletter.

"What a coincidence," Pat winked as he turned to me.

I couldn't help but smile back. "I had a really good time this evening," I told him.

"Me too," he said.

Chapter 14

A couple of days later, the activities department had a ladies-only group. We were getting our nails done. Anna, Ila, Denise, and I all decided to join in on the manicure, as we were all desperate for one.

"All hail the queen," Anna said with a laugh as I came into the room.

"What?" I asked, having no idea what she was talking about.

"The queen," Anna said. "You're the Prom Queen."

"Oh yeah," I said, blushing. "You should have been the queen."

"No, no. I've been the queen before, a couple of times actually," Anna said. "I have no desire to be the queen again. My reign is over," she said with a dramatic flair.

"It was nice that it was you and Pat," Denise said.

"To tell you the truth, it was a little embarrassing," I said.

"Why?" asked Ila. "He's a nice gentleman."

"Oh, I know that," I said. "It's just that—"

"It's just that you kind of like him," Anna said.

"He's a friend," I said.

"That you like," Anna said, attempting to finish my sentence.

"Okay, okay, I do think he's nice and I like his personality," I said. "But it's too soon after Larry. I can't see myself coupling up with anyone just yet. I'm still grieving my husband."

"That's fair," Denise said.

"That doesn't mean you're blind to other men, Judith. Larry would want you to be happy. If spending time with Pat, being friends with Pat, is making you happy, then that's okay," Anna said.

"Well, when you put it that way, I suppose it makes sense," I said.

"I always make sense," Anna said.

"How did your appointment go yesterday?" Ila asked Anna.

I had forgotten all about Anna's appointment. It was her first chemotherapy treatment. I felt a little guilty for not having asked earlier and making the conversation about myself.

"It went just fine," Anna said, with a smile. "No worries."

"Who went with you?" Denise asked.

"My daughter, Kristin," Anna replied. "She's an RN, so she knows her stuff."

"That's good," said Ila. "You're lucky to have her."

"I know," said Anna. "She told those other nurses they better take good care of me," she laughed.

I had to laugh with her. With Anna, laughter and smiling seemed to do her more good than anything else.

The next day, Pat and his aide arrived at my door around three o'clock. Pat said he just wanted to know if I'd like to come out to the front patio and sit outside with him for a bit. It was a nice, sunny afternoon, a good day for it. I told him sure.

The aide took both Pat and I outside on the front patio of Pine Meadows to sit in the sunshine and get some fresh air. It felt refreshing. I thanked Pat for the suggestion.

"Oh, you're very welcome," he said. "I come out here a lot this time of year, if anything, just to get outside of those four walls."

"That makes sense. I can see why. It's peaceful out here," I said.

"Judith, can I ask you a personal question?" Pat prompted.

Oh no, I was afraid of where he was going with this. This could be anything. I was scared to find out. I wanted to scream No and run back inside the building, but there was no aide to assist me back inside at the moment.

"Um, sure," I said.

"Do you ever miss Larry so much that it keeps you awake at night? That's how I feel about my Betty sometimes. That's how I felt last night. I just kept thinking about all of our good memories and the life that we had, and I couldn't sleep, didn't want to sleep."

I wasn't expecting him to ask that, or admit that.

"Yes, I do feel the same. I miss Larry so much that I spend time day or night thinking about the best times of our lives, even the worse times of our lives that we always conquered together."

Pat just nodded.

We sat in silence for a little while, just basking in the sun and enjoying each other's company. After a while, I looked over and noticed that Pat had closed his eyes and fallen asleep. I wasn't about to disturb him, but thought I would just continue to sit in the sun and enjoy getting lost in my own thoughts for a while.

But then a vehicle pulled into the front parking lot that I recognized. It was Carolyn's. I was glad she was there for a visit, but a bit bummed that my outdoor time would be coming to an end.

As Carolyn walked up to the front patio, I noticed that Cindy was with her—what a nice surprise to see them both!

Pat woke up upon hearing them and sat up a little bit straighter in his wheelchair.

"Well, hello Mother," Carolyn said. "We weren't expecting to find you out here today."

"Oh, it's such a nice day," I said. "Pat asked me if I wanted to come sit outside and I took him up on the offer. Oh, where are my manners! Carolyn and Cindy, this is Pat DeWalter. Pat, these are my daughters, Carolyn and Cindy."

"Nice to meet you," Pat said.

"Likewise," Carolyn said.

"Nice to meet you as well," Cindy said.

"Mom, why don't we go inside to visit? Is that okay?" Carolyn asked.

"Sure," I said. It made no difference to me.

After finding an aide to assist me back to my room, Carolyn, Cindy, and I settled in for our visit. I was hoping they had some good news as far as my return back home.

"So how is everything at the house?" I asked.

"Everything is good," Carolyn said. "We still need to keep downsizing. We'll need to bring you home for another day to work on getting rid of some things."

"I don't want to get rid of too many things if I'm going to be going back there to live Carolyn."

Carolyn sighed, "We need to talk about that Mother. We still haven't found anyone who can stay with you at night. We're working on it, but please understand that it might not happen right away, if ever."

"I don't need anyone to stay with me at night, Carolyn. No one stays with me at night here. And when I press my call button, it takes them over thirty minutes to answer it anyway. I could call one of you in the night if I needed something and you could answer within thirty minutes just the same," I said.

"That's not the same as if there were an emergency," Cindy said.

"Emergencies can happen to anyone," I said. "That's what 911 is for."

"Let's just wait and see if we can find someone who can stay at night. I would feel a lot better about that. In the meantime, we do still need to downsize and declutter, Mom," Carolyn said. "I'll speak with the staff here about when would be a good day for us to take you home again."

"Okay," I said, with a sigh.

"Something else we need to talk about," Carolyn began. "This gentleman, Pat, how close are the two of you? I saw in the Pine Meadows newsletter that you two were the King and Queen of the prom and now just saw the two of you spending time together out on the front patio. What's that all about?"

"We're just friends," I said. "He's a nice gentleman. We have some nice conversations is all."

"You know Mom, Dad just passed away. It really seems a bit too soon to be looking into another relationship with someone," Cindy said.

"Oh, no, Cindy, that's not it at all," I said. "I'm not in a relationship with Pat. We're just friends, I promise."

"Are you sure he knows that, Mother?" Carolyn asked.

"Yes, I am positive. We talk about your father and Pat's late wife all the time," I said.

"I'll be honest, I just don't want to see you getting into another relationship so soon after Dad's passing," Carolyn said.

"You don't have to worry dear. Pat is simply my friend," I clarified.

Chapter 15

The following day was another therapy day. This time I had Rob as my therapist again.

Rob had good news. Sammy had talked to Jill about my concerns about my therapy being too

easy and, since I hadn't had any falls recently, Jill had upgraded my therapy to higher intensity-

based goals. I was excited, and Rob was too.

Rob had me work in something called the parallel bars on some higher-level balance

exercises. The parallel bars were just there to hold on to something if need be. Rob had me stand

on pieces of foam and reach for cones outside of my comfort zone, as well as walk on foam

sideways and backward. It was challenging, but in a good way. Rob also had me pick cones up

from the floor and weave my way through a cone obstacle course, as if I were navigating clutter

at home. He also had me practice walking sideways with my walker, to simulate how I would

need to walk in and out of my half bathroom at home.

When we were almost done with our session, I asked him if I could please practice

walking up and down the stairs. He told me that Jill did add that as one of my goals and that he

was willing to give it a try if I was. Boy, was I excited.

So, Rob and I walked over to the makeshift staircase. There were four smaller stairs on

one side and three larger stairs on the other side. Rob suggested I start with the four smaller

stairs, and I agreed. We headed to that end and I set my walker off to the side. I reached for both

handrails and placed one foot up onto the first step. With all of my might, and a little boost from

Rob, I hoisted my body up onto the first step. After that, I made my way up to the second step,

the third, and then the fourth. I turned around and slowly lowered myself down each one with

Rob's help.

I was ecstatic! It did take Rob's assistance, but I walked up and down the steps! I couldn't wait to tell Carolyn and Cindy. I knew that the more I practiced, the less and less I would need his help and that soon enough I would be able to go up and down those steps on my own. I thanked Rob profusely for his help and couldn't wait to share the good news with Anna, Ila, and Denise at lunchtime.

But at lunchtime that day, Denise and Ila were the only ones there.

"Anna's in the hospital," Denise said.

"Why?" I asked. I was her roommate and I didn't even know.

"She's got some sort of infection," Denise said. "It doesn't sound good."

"We should pray for her," Ila said.

"What kind of infection?" I asked.

"A respiratory infection," Denise said. "She's in the ICU."

"Oh my," I said. "Yes, we should pray for her. What are they doing for her?"

"I don't know," Denise said. "I just caught Kristin in the hallway as she was getting a few of Anna's things earlier."

We ate most of our meal in silence. It wasn't the time for me to bring up my success in therapy. It just wasn't the same without Anna, the most talkative one of the group. All of us were looking forward to having her back and couldn't wait for her to beat this respiratory infection.

When I got back to my room, things were pretty quiet. Anna usually had her television up fairly loud, and now it was silent. I was also used to her yelling at it when she didn't agree with something, and now there was no yelling. It made me sad. I said a quick prayer for Anna for healing. I wanted her and her fun-loving spirit to return as soon as possible.

The next day I woke, hoping to hear some news on Anna. As soon as my aide arrived to help me get ready for the day, I asked her if she had heard anything on Anna's condition.

"Nope, and I'm not allowed to say anything even if I did. HIPAA, you know," she said.

At breakfast, Ila and Denise appeared to be just as worried as I was.

"Have you heard anything?" I asked them both as I sat down at the table.

"Not yet," Denise said.

"But we're still praying," Ila said.

"Of course, me too," I said.

Lunchtime and dinnertime came and there was still no word on Anna's condition. The days came and went and none of us heard anything. Then approximately four days later, Anna's daughter, Kristin, came in to get a few more things from Anna's room. The curtains happened to be opened and I couldn't help but ask her how my dear friend was doing.

"Kristin?" I poked my head around the corner from my recliner chair.

"Yes?" she answered.

"Hi, I'm Judith. I'm a good friend of Anna's. I'm just wondering how she's doing."

"Hi Judith. She's not doing very well. Her cancer has metastasized, despite the chemotherapy. She's coming back to Pine Meadows, but she's transitioning to hospice today."

I gasped. Anna? Hospice? I never would have dreamed of it.

"If there's anything I can do, please let me know," I said.

I didn't know what else to say.

"Thank you," she said, as she gathered the few things she came for and left the room.

The following day, Anna returned to Pine Meadows. I could hear the buzz of activity behind the curtain. I could hear Anna talking—she sounded like her usual peppy self, not someone who was on hospice. Pretty soon, the activity died down and the television was on with the volume turned up, Anna-style.

I pressed my call button for an aide to help me walk over to visit with Anna. As soon as the aide arrived, we walked behind the curtains.

"Anna?" I prodded.

"What?" She asked, as if I was interrupting her favorite television program.

"How are you doing?"

"I'm doing fine. Why? What did Kristin tell you?" she asked.'

"She said that you were on hospice now," I replied.

"That girl, always spreading my business." Anna shook her head. "Yes, I'm on hospice," she said matter-of-factly.

"Oh Anna, I'm so sorry—"

"Stop right there," she said. "Have you told the others?"

"No, not yet."

"Please don't. I don't want anyone to know I'm dying. You hear?"

It was a tall order, and a big secret to keep. I wasn't sure I could do it. But if it was Anna's final wish, I supposed I could honor it.

"Okay, Anna," I said.

As the weeks went on, however, Anna's condition began to deteriorate. She went from being able to take meals in the dining hall to having to take meals in her room. The other ladies could tell that something was wrong.

"Anna's getting worse," Ila said one evening at dinner.

"I heard they called hospice in," Denise said.

I just kept my mouth shut.

"You're awfully quiet, Judith," Denise said. "Does she ever say anything to you, as your roommate and all?"

I hated lying to them, but I wanted to honor Anna's wishes as well.

"I know her health is going downhill," I said.

"We should ask to go down and visit her after dinner this evening," Ila said.

"That's a good idea," Denise said.

After dinner, when the aides were coming around to take us back to our rooms, Ila and Denise asked to go to Anna's room for a visit. They were told that they weren't allowed in Anna's room at that time and I was told I wasn't allowed to go back to my room temporarily, either.

"Why not?" I asked.

"Because Anna has just passed away," the aide stated. "We'll be back for you when you can go back to your room, but it might be a while."

I found myself in a state of shock. One of my best friends since I came to Pine Meadows was gone. I'd be going to a second funeral in a matter of months. That's the worst part about getting older, grieving more and grieving harder. I supposed I would have to ask Carolyn to bring my funeral clothes in to Pine Meadows. Getting older just wasn't fair.

Denise let out a sob, interrupting my thoughts.

Ila gave her a hug, "It's okay, she's in a better place now."

"She was my best friend," Denise cried.

"I know," Ila said, holding Denise tighter.

"She sure was an amazing person," I said. "I was blessed to know her."

We spent the rest of the evening sharing memories of Anna with each other. Denise told of a time when her blood sugar was low and the nurse insisted on giving her insulin. Denise was trying to tell the nurse that she needed a snack instead to increase her blood sugar, but the nurse wasn't listening. Finally, Anna stepped up and said that if the nurse didn't listen to Denise, Anna was going to report the issue to the Resident Council. So, Denise got the snack that she needed and her blood sugar was elevated to the appropriate level.

Ila told of a time when her portable oxygen tank was running low on oxygen and she reported it to one of the aides in the dining hall, but the aide didn't do anything about it. Ila said that she told Anna that she was having difficulty breathing as her tank was empty and no one would replace it. Ila said that Anna wheeled herself over to the storage unit where the tanks were located and told the aides that she was going to find a way to break in if they didn't hurry up and get in there and get a tank for Ila. Needless to say, Ila got a new tank.

I, of course, just shared how friendly Anna had been when I first arrived at Pine Meadows and that she had immediately welcomed me into her group of friends, Ila and Denise. I shared how appreciative I was of that, since I hadn't been too keen on coming to Pine Meadows in the first place. Having a group of friends from the get-go was a lifesaver, and it was all thanks to Anna.

That night in my room was another quiet night, but this time it was Anna who was on my mind. She was never coming back. I had gotten used to her loud television and occasional commentary. She was a good roommate. Occasionally we would banter back and forth through the curtains just for something to do. That was all over now. I wondered who my next roommate would be and what she would be like. Would I be as welcoming to her as Anna had been to me? I hoped so, although I couldn't imagine anyone taking Anna's place in our friendship group.

A couple of days later, Carolyn and Cindy arrived to pick me up for another trip back home. I was really looking forward to this one. After all of the therapy I'd been doing, I was sure this trip would go well. The girls were more focused on all of the sorting we had to do rather than the things I wanted to do, which was practice navigating throughout the house.

When we arrived home, I noticed that there wasn't nearly as much clutter as there had been the last time I was there. The girls must have sorted through a lot without me. I wasn't sure why they brought me back at all if they were going to sort through some things without me. It looked like the girls had already gone through most of Larry's things.

"It looks like you've already gone through some things," I said.

"We had to get a head start Mom, otherwise we'd be way behind," Carolyn said.

"You should have let me be the one to go through your father's things," I said.

"There's still more of his things to go through," Cindy said.

"You should have let me go through all of his things," I said.

"Let's try not to get worked up here Mom. There's still a lot of work to do," Carolyn said.

I tried my best to remain calm. After all, she was the one who was going to make the decision whether or not I stayed at Pine Meadows.

"Okay, let's get to work," I said.

So, we started sorting. We made piles labeled junk, save, and not sure. My not sure pile was pretty high, however, and Carolyn soon put a stop to that.

"From now on we're only going to have junk and save piles. And your junk pile has to be higher than your save pile, okay?"

That was a tall order, but I was up for the task. We worked for hours separating piles of stuff. I hated putting anything of Larry's into a junk pile, but I was happy with what I saved. I found a couple of items that belonged with the lock box that I put in my purse to take back to Pine Meadows.

After we were done sorting for the day—we had made some headway, but still had a way to go—I decided to take a walk around the house just to prove to myself that I could do it. I used my walker, and walked from the living room to the dining room to the kitchen with no trouble whatsoever this time. I also navigated my way to the half bathroom and practiced walking in sideways with my walker, just like Rob and I practiced in therapy. It went very well. I even turned to sit on the toilet with ease. I made sure Carolyn was watching my every move so that she was aware that I could do it. I knew I wasn't quite ready to tackle the steps without help just yet, but told her that was coming along as I had done them in therapy with Rob.

She seemed impressed. However, she reminded me that we didn't have anyone who could stay with me at night. She said that she and Cindy were still working on that. And that if they could come up with something feasible, it could be possible for me to come home. I was elated. She said in the meantime, however, they did have to continue to prepare as if I was going to stay at Pine Meadows and keep organizing the house. I said I understood. I would pray for someone to come along to stay with me at night.

Back at Pine Meadows, the activity of the day was another card game. This time it was Tripoly and again Pat was at my table. I was much more adept at Tripoly than Skip-Bo, so I didn't need nearly as much instruction, but it was nice to have Pat by my side. We conversed throughout the game, as usual.

"I'm sorry to hear about your friend Anna," Pat said.

"Thank you," I said. "She was a great woman."

"Yes, she was always the life of the party," he said with a smile.

I laughed also. "Yes, she was."

"Do you have a new roommate yet?" he asked.

"Not yet. They say I'm supposed to get one either today or tomorrow."

"That will be interesting. I hope it's someone nice for your sake," he said.

"I'll have to take what I get I suppose," I said.

"How was your trip home the other day?"

"My what?"

"Your visit home—with your daughters, to sort out items," he said.

"Oh yes, it went well. We sorted through quite a lot. I managed to navigate through the house without falling," I said, with a laugh.

"That's good!" Pat said.

"Any word from Dave?" I asked.

"No, not since he told me my grandson was deploying into the Navy. He's busy though, with the family and work."

I was sorry I brought that up.

"Are you going to sit outside after the activities today?" I asked.

"Yes, would you care to join me?"

"I'd love to," I said.

That evening, there was some commotion across the curtains from my room to Anna's old room. My new roommate was moving in. I tried to listen in as best I could to learn her name and as much as I could about her, but there was a lot going on. Whoever she was, she had a lot of family. Finally, things started to calm down a bit and I heard one of them call her Norma. However, by the time all of her family members left, it was too late at night for me to call for an aide to help me over to introduce myself. I hoped Norma wouldn't think I was being rude. I would have to wait and introduce myself in the morning.

The next morning, after my aide assisted me to get ready for the day, I asked her to walk me over to greet and introduce myself to Norma. She took me across to the curtains, where I saw a very frail, older woman who appeared to be in her late nineties, sitting up in her recliner chair reading her Bible.

"Hello, my name is Judith. I'm your roommate across the curtains here. I wanted to introduce myself last night, but it was getting late," I said.

"Hello, Judith. My name is Norma. It's nice to meet you."

"It's nice to meet you as well, Norma," I said. "You're welcome to sit with my friends and me at mealtime if you'd like. Just look for me. I'll save you a seat just in case."

"Oh, thank you for the offer dear, but I'll likely be eating my meals here in my room. I'm not much for going out," she said.

She was nice, but other than that, she was the polar opposite of Anna, I could tell.

"Okay, I understand. But if you change your mind, you know you can look for me," I said.

"Thank you, dear," she said.

I made my way back to my room, a bit disheartened. I wanted someone who was more outgoing, fun loving, and spirited. Let's face it, I wanted Anna back, just like I wanted Larry back. It wasn't fair. I was losing everyone I loved and grieving was difficult. No one could take the place of my husband and best friend.

Chapter 16

If there's one thing I'd learned over the past couple of months, it's that time doesn't wait around for anyone. There were still things I wanted to accomplish in my life, and I knew I needed to accomplish them now, instead of waiting around for the right time.

I had my opportunity for that the following week in activities when we were all encouraged to write a letter to a family member. The activities staff said that we could write to whoever we wanted to and that if we didn't know the address, they would help us track it down. I wondered just how serious they were about that, but as I thought of the lock box I got to work composing my letter, one that I've been wanting to send for over sixty years.

Dear Baby Girl,

I don't know if you wish to hear from me. I don't know if you've ever wished to hear from me. I hope you've had a spectacular life with Rick and Sonya Grime. They seemed like the perfect couple when Larry and I had to give you up for adoption in 1958. I hope you were able to go to a good school and get a good education. ~~Larry and I went on to have two other daughters later in life, so you have two sisters that maybe someday you could meet.~~ Larry recently passed away from a heart attack, I'm sorry to say. And I'm currently in a nursing home, called Pine Meadows, but I'm looking forward to hopefully returning home soon. I'd like to know more about you and what your life has been like, if you'll allow it. I've thought about you day and night since the day Larry and I had to hand you over to Rick and Sonya. Although I know it was for the best, we were so young, only sixteen, ~~I still wonder what life would have been like if we could have kept you with us,~~ I still have a lock box of a few of your items from the day you were born. I have your identification bracelet, the onesie you wore your first day in the hospital, and, surprisingly, a lock of your hair, as you had a full head of thick brown hair when you were born.

I treasure these items and even have them with me here at Pine Meadows, as I wouldn't want

anything to happen to them. I guess what I'm trying to say with this letter is that time is passing

faster every day, especially for me, and I'm hoping that you might be willing to meet me. I live at

Pine Meadows (the address is on the return address on the envelope) in room 422-A. I

understand if you're too busy at this time or maybe just not interested or willing to meet me.

These issues are difficult and, especially back then, can be tough for a child. But I would be

overjoyed to see you again after all these years.

Love,

Judith March

I did have great difficulty writing the letter. I went over it probably one hundred times. I
was the last person in the activities room when everyone else had finished writing their letters.

"Judith, are you finished?" Kathy, the activities staff member, asked.

"Yes, I think so. You said you would help find the addresses of anyone, correct?"

"Yes, we'll do the best we can," she said.

"Well, this letter is to my daughter who I gave up for adoption when she was born in
1958. I know she went with a family, Rick and Sonya Grime, but my daughter would be sixty-
two years old by now and I don't know her name."

"Oh my," Kathy said. "This is a bit of a tall order. But let's see what we can do. We
might have to make some phone calls and do some investigating. It might take a while Judith."

"I understand," I said.

Later that day, at lunchtime, the ladies and I were discussing the activities group.

"You looked like you were pretty intense there Judith," Denise said.

"Yeah, who were you writing to?" Ila asked.

"My daughter," I said.

"Carolyn?" Denise asked.

"No," I said. I had never told them about the daughter I had given up for adoption. I guessed there was no time like the present, especially if there was a chance she might come visit me at Pine Meadows.

"I wrote to my first-born daughter, who I gave up for adoption when Larry and I were just sixteen. I haven't seen her or spoken to her since the day she was born. I'm hoping to meet her," I said.

Ila gasped, "Oh my, that's been on your heart all these years, I can't even imagine."

"I just hope that the activities staff can track her down. That's not really their job," I said.

"If they can't track her down, we'll help you," Denise said. "My daughter works in the family court system. I'm sure there's something she could do to help you find your daughter."

"Oh, thank you Denise. That is so kind of you," I said.

That night, back in my room, all I could think about was my baby girl. I opened the lock box and looked at her precious items, all that I had of her. With tears in my eyes, I imagined what it would be like to meet her again. Of course, she would be an adult, but a well-adjusted one I hoped. I sighed; it would be a while until I would find out, if at all.

Then, Anna's television turned on, as usual for this hour. I realized I hadn't told her yet about my daughter that I had given up for adoption and that I was planning to meet her soon, hopefully here at Pine Meadows.

It was too late to ask for an aide to take me across the curtains, so I decided to just holler, as Anna and I sometimes did.

"Hey, Anna!" I called.

No answer.

"Anna!" I called again.

No answer again.

Maybe she didn't have her hearing aids in.

"Anna!" I shouted.

Still, no answer.

That was odd. Maybe she fell asleep with the television on.

The following day, Pat asked me to sit outside with him. It was a sunny day and about seventy-five degrees, in my opinion, ideal for relaxing outside. Our aides wheeled us both out to the front patio and we sat side by side in the sun just enjoying each other's company.

The subject of yesterday's activity session came up. Pat said he wrote his letter to his grandson who was shipping off to the Navy. He said he wanted to tell him how proud he was of him and how much he loved him before he left. He asked me who I wrote my letter to, if I didn't mind him asking.

I told him that I wrote my letter to my first-born daughter that Larry and I had given up for adoption when we were sixteen. I told him the whole story about how disappointed our parents had been at the time and had wanted to send me away throughout my pregnancy, but decided against it when Larry and I agreed that we would give the baby up for adoption. We had found a nice couple, Rick and Sonya, however, they wanted a closed adoption, which meant that we would not have any involvement with the baby what so ever after the baby was born. Our parents were all in agreement that that was for the best.

So, when the time came to give birth to the baby, Rick and Sonya were at the hospital to hold her as soon as she was born. I didn't get the chance. I told Pat that I was lucky to get the items I did that I had placed in the lock box: the precious ID bracelet, onesie, and lock of hair. I only received those items out of the goodness of the Grime's hearts. I told Pat that Larry and I rarely spoke about the baby girl. I thought it was just too heart breaking for Larry, both at the time and ever since then to bring it up. Now that Larry was gone, and Anna, both so quickly, I was realizing how precious life is and how fast it passes by. I wanted to try to connect with my daughter while I still had the chance. And if she said no, at least I could say that I tried.

"You've been carrying a heavy load Judith," Pat said. "I do hope that you are able to connect with your daughter. That would be wonderful, for both of you."

"Denise said her daughter might be able to help me," I said. "Even if the activities staff can't find the correct address, I want to make sure my letter gets to her somehow."

"That would be great," Pat said. He gave me a genuine smile. "You deserve to meet your daughter Judith. I bet she's turned out to be an amazing woman."

"Thank you," I smiled back.

The next day, I ran into Kathy on my way down to lunch. She stopped my aide and me to deliver some news.

"Good news Judith, we were able to find an address for the agency that took care of the adoption. We're one step closer to delivering your letter!"

"What letter?" I asked.

She looked at me quizzically, "The letter you wrote yesterday in activities."

"I didn't write any letter," I laughed.

"Yes, you did," she said. "You wrote a letter to your daughter that you gave up for adoption several years ago. You wanted us to find the correct address to deliver it to her."

"I did not!" I said. "How do you know anything about that?" I burst into tears.

She had no right to invade my privacy like that. Did she find the lockbox in my room? Were they searching our rooms now? No one knew about my adopted daughter. How did Kathy find out? I was scared. There was some kind of conspiracy going on around here. And I didn't like it one bit.

Chapter 17

A couple of days later, Carolyn and Cindy came for a visit. Their demeanor was different than usual. It was like they were walking on eggshells around me, and being very careful what they said. Finally, I'd had enough.

"Okay, what's the deal, girls?" I asked. "Why are you treating me like I'm going to shatter into pieces at any moment?"

"Mother, there's something we have to talk about, and I'm not sure you're going to like it," Carolyn said.

"Oh, great," I said, sarcastically.

"It's not a laughing matter," she said. "The staff here said they've been noticing that you've been getting more forgetful about some things."

"Forgetful?" I asked. "Me?"

"Yes," Cindy said. "They said you're forgetting things that you've done the next day, and sometimes just hours after doing them."

"Like what?" I asked.

"They didn't give us the specifics," Carolyn said. "But they're concerned. They think you might be going through the early stages of dementia."

"Dementia? Now that's absurd. If there's one thing I do not have to worry about, it's dementia," I said.

"The staff says that sometimes you try to cover it with anger," Carolyn said softly.

"Girls, you both know me better than that. As much as life has kicked me in the pants, it takes a lot for me to get angry. You know that, right?" I pleaded. I knew I didn't have dementia.

"True," Cindy said.

"Maybe we need to take another visit home," Carolyn said. "Not to sort anything, but just to have a nice visit at home for the day. Maybe that would help take your mind off of things. What do you say?"

We agreed to another home visit in two days. I couldn't wait.

A couple of days later, an aide came around to get me ready for the outing.

"Where am I going?" I asked.

"You're going for a visit home with your daughters," she said.

"I am? When did this come about?"

"They signed you out in the books a couple of days ago," she said.

"Well I wish they would have told me about it," I said.

Before Carolyn and Cindy arrived, I opened my nightstand drawer and took one more look at the lockbox. I really hoped the activities department would be able to make some headway with the letter. It seemed like everywhere I went lately, people were teaming up against me. I desperately wanted to meet my daughter. I put the lockbox back in the drawer right as Carolyn and Cindy arrived at my door.

"You two could have mentioned this surprise outing," I laughed.

They exchanged a glance, but didn't say anything.

"I mean, it was a nice surprise. I'm looking forward to going home," I said.

"Mother, we did discuss it, when we came to visit you two days ago," Carolyn said softly. "Don't you remember?"

She was obviously lying, trying to make me seem like a feeble, forgetful old woman. I wasn't going to let her have that satisfaction.

"Maybe you think you discussed it with me, but you conveniently forgot to mention it," I snapped.

Again, Carolyn and Cindy exchanged a look, but said nothing. Cindy was always pretty docile when it came to confrontations and let her sister take the lead.

"But all is well, I'm glad to be going home," I said.

"Okay, Mother, let's head home," Carolyn said.

After we made it to the house, I noticed there were still piles of items that needed sorted through, but Carolyn said we weren't going to sort through those this time. She cooked one of my favorite meals—ham loaf and whipped potatoes with green beans, the kind of food they don't serve at Pine Meadows, and we just sat and chatted for hours. The entire day was a nice visit, until Carolyn came out with it.

"Mom, we made you a doctor's appointment."

"A doctor's appointment? For what? I'm not sick."

"We just want a doctor to check your memory," she said.

"My memory? My memory is just fine. I can remember things from all the way back when I was a child, crystal clear," I said.

"We're more worried about what you can remember from day to day right now," Cindy blurted out.

"I remember just fine. I remember you girls forcing me out of this house and making me live at Pine Meadows after your father died," I said.

"Will you please just go to the doctor, if for anything, just to prove us wrong?" Carolyn said.

"Fine," I relented.

Carolyn made a doctor's appointment with Dr. Stanbery for the following Friday. She, Cindy, and I all loaded up and went to Dr. Stanbery's office for my appointment. I wasn't overly excited, but I was looking forward to proving them wrong. There was nothing wrong with my brain or my memory.

When we arrived for the appointment, Dr. Stanbery had me look at a series of cards and try to remember three words. He said he was going to ask me what those three words were later on during the test, so it was very important that I remember those three words. Then, he asked me to count backwards from one hundred by sevens. That was difficult! I had to think about that and missed a couple. He asked me to spell the word world backward, and I spelled it D-L-O-R-W, instead of D-L-R-O-W. He did a couple more tests that I barely passed, but by the time it was over, I was so flustered I could only remember two of the three words he had asked me to remember. I hoped this was the average grade most people got on this kind of test, because it was challenging.

Dr. Stanbery left the room for a while and didn't come back for a long period of time. When he finally did return, he had a graph chart with him. He held it up and started talking about my score on the test. He said that my score was in the range of the curve that placed me in the mild dementia category. He said there was good news and bad news. The bad news was that my dementia would likely progress as I got older, but the good news was that there was a new medication we could try to combat the progression of the dementia if I was willing to try it.

I expected Carolyn to pipe up with a "See, told ya so, Mom!" but she didn't. Both she and Cindy were waiting for me to respond.

"How do you know for sure I have dementia, Dr. Stanbery, and that I'm just not a good test taker?" I asked.

"That's a good question, Judith. This particular test has been researched heavily across the world. The statistics have proven that it's one of the best at determining levels of dementia in elderly patients. We wouldn't use this test if the research hadn't proven it to be one of the best."

"But, Dr. Stanbery, I feel fine. I don't feel like I have dementia."

"Most patients do feel fine, Judith. Dementia is not a disease you feel. It's a disease that, unfortunately, attacks your brain and how you think. What do you say about that medication? Do you want to give it a try?"

"I suppose," I said grudgingly.

So, we left the doctor's office, prescription in hand, headed to the pharmacy, and then back to Pine Meadows. Carolyn and Cindy checked me in and handed the prescription bottle over to the staff. They explained the doctor's visit to the nursing staff and handed over some paperwork. My aide took me back to my room where I took a nap. It had been a long day.

Chapter 18

The next day in activities, Kathy told me that she had been able to contact the adoption agency that took care of my baby girl's adoption to Rick and Sonya Grime. She told me that she had some exciting news and asked if I wanted to come to her office to talk about it. I told her of course.

Once settled in Kathy's office. Kathy told me that Rick and Sonya had named the baby girl Linda and that they had moved to El Paso, Texas. She said that Rick had worked as a postal worker and Sonya was a stay-at-home mom who cared for Linda around the clock. She said she did not know where Rick, Sonya, or Linda were currently living or if any of them were still living, but she had high hopes that Linda would still be alive since she would only be in her sixties. Kathy said that was the most that the adoption agency could give her, but that it was more information than we had before.

I was elated to know that my baby girl had a name: Linda. What a beautiful name. I loved it. I couldn't think of a better name for her. Linda Grime. Of course, she had probably gotten married and her last name was different now, but Linda Grime was lovely. I knew I would have to seek Denise's help if I were to go any further in my search. I thanked Kathy for her assistance.

That evening, at dinnertime, I sat with Ila and Denise and filled them in on how the search was going so far and what Kathy had been able to dig up from the adoption agency.

"Do you still think your daughter might be able to help me?" I asked Denise.

"Of course! That's what she does for a living," Denise said.

"Oh, thank you, that would just mean the world to me," I said.

"That's very kind of you Denise," Ila said. "I wish I could help you more. I look forward to meeting your daughter though, when she comes to Pine Meadows, Judith."

That night, I went to bed dreaming of Linda Grime and the day I would get to meet her. Hopefully she would want to meet me. Hopefully she wouldn't think that Larry and I had just gotten rid of her. We would never do that. With any luck, I would get to meet her and explain the whole situation. The only part I hadn't thought through was introducing her to Carolyn and Cindy. They didn't know they had an older sister. That might be a bit of an issue. But the thought of meeting Linda Grime meant more to me than anything at the moment. I fell asleep peacefully.

The next morning, at breakfast, Denise said that her daughter was already in search of Linda Grime in the family court system. She said she might not be able to come up with any more information than the adoption agency had, but she would try. I thanked Denise profusely for being so prompt in asking her daughter for help.

Later that day, it was time for another therapy session. I arrived at the therapy gym to find Rob as my therapist that day. I was determined to do a good job, as I wanted to be in top-notch shape when I met Linda Grime. I asked him to put me through the paces.

"We can do that," he laughed.

He put me in the parallel bars and had me do tandem-stance walking on foam, which is basically like tight-rope walking on a narrower base of foam, single leg stance on a piece of foam, tip toe walking, heel walking, balancing on a balance board, side-stepping on foam, walking backward on foam, picking up cones from the ground, and the dreaded squats, in perfect form as Rob always insisted.

After we finished all of this, we headed over to the stairs. Rob said it was best to practice the stairs when my legs were fatigued, as there were going to be times at home when I would need to go up and down the stairs when I was tired. He was right. I asked Rob if we could practice the taller set of stairs this time, instead of the smaller set, as mine at home were more like the taller stairs. He agreed.

We made our way over to the taller set of stairs and I placed my walker off to the side. Rob held on to my gait belt for safety's sake as I placed my foot up onto the first step. I held onto both handrails and used all of my might to hoist myself up onto the first step and bring my other foot up.

"Did you help?" I asked.

"No, I didn't, Judith. You did that all on your own. Let's see if you can make it to the top!"

There were two more steps to go to make it to the to platform. I braced myself and hoisted myself up onto the second step and then the third. Once I was on the platform, I turned around and looked at Rob.

"Did you help me at all?" I asked.

"All I did was hold your gait belt," Rob said with a smile.

I grinned. I did it! I stepped down the stairs one at a time with ease, with Rob watching closely. I was exhausted, but I was one step closer to tackling my steps at home. Rob gave me a high five.

After therapy, I was in a great mood. I didn't see how I could possibly have dementia when things were going so great for me. But if Dr. Stanbery was right, maybe this new medication would help, and things would go even better. I couldn't wait to talk to Denise that evening at dinner to see what her daughter may have found out regarding Linda.

That evening, Denise said that her daughter had found a bit of information that I might find useful. She said that although Linda Grime had grown up in El Paso, Texas, she no longer lived there. She lived in Oklahoma City, Oklahoma. She didn't have any information on Rick and Sonya, but Denise said that her daughter did have an address for Linda. She wasn't sure if it was a current address or not, but said it was the best she could do.

Denise gave me the address and I thanked her profusely. Although Anna had been the leader of our group, Denise was a great friend. I had never given her enough credit in the past and was now feeling guilty about that. She would do anything for anyone. She had such a caring heart.

The next day in activities was another balloon volleyball game. This time I was matched up with Pat. As soon as I saw Kathy, though, I asked him if we could take a time-out. He agreed. I had Linda's address in my pocket.

"Kathy?" I called out.

"Yes, Judith?"

"My friend Denise did some investigating and we believe we have an address for my baby girl, for Linda Grime. I wanted to give it to you so you could send the letter."

"That's great, Judith! I'll take it. All we can do is pray, right?" she said.

"Right," I agreed.

And I went back to playing balloon volleyball with Pat.

Chapter 19

Weeks went by with no word back from Linda Grime. I resigned myself to the fact that maybe we had the wrong address, but the letter hadn't been returned to sender. I went about my normal routines at Pine Meadows: spending time with Ila and Denise, going to activities, getting my hair and nails done, playing cards with Pat, and taking the occasional trip home with Carolyn and Cindy. I couldn't tell if my new medicine was working or not, but Carolyn and Cindy seemed happy, so that's all that mattered, other than finding Linda Grime.

I was sitting in my room one day, reading a book I had checked out from the Pine Meadows library, when everything changed. Kathy from activities came around and said I had mail. I never got mail. Everyone I knew was close enough to visit me. But here I was, getting mail. She had a big smile on her face as she delivered the envelope. I looked at the return address. It was from Oklahoma City! I tore open the envelope.

Dear Judith,

It was wonderful to hear from you, as I have wanted to for so long. I just wasn't quite sure how to go about searching for you and knew you probably had a family of your own by now and didn't want to interfere. I want you to know that Rick and Sonya were wonderful parents to me. I had a delightful childhood, full of happiness and love. I was an only child, so they doted on me quite a bit.

They did not tell me I was adopted until my eighteenth birthday. I must say, it came as quite a shock and I had a lot of questions at that time. They wouldn't tell me about you and Larry, just said that my birth parents were very young and not able to raise a child at such a young age. This I understood, as I had a couple of friends of my own in the 1970s who were pregnant and very ill equipped to raise their children on their own.

I am sad to say that both of my parents have passed away. My father passed away from lung cancer in 2002 and my mother passed away from Alzheimer's disease in 2017. It was a trying time, to say the least. I am currently living on my own in Oklahoma City after going through a nasty divorce in 2009. I don't wish to go through something like that again, so I don't put myself out there, if you know what I mean. I don't have any children, but I do have two dogs, Rocco and Sadie. They are my babies.

I would love to meet up with you sometime. I have so many questions I'd love to ask you. And I'd love to see if we look alike, silly I know. You said you were at Pine Meadows. That's the nursing home in Bedford Hills, Michigan, correct? I'm sure I can coordinate a flight and a hotel; it just might take me a while to make all of the arrangements. Please write me back if that's something you are interested in.

Thank you again for your letter. It brought tears to my eyes as I have been waiting for it for several years.

With Love,

Linda Grime

I closed Linda's letter and started to cry, happy tears of course. I held her letter close to my heart. Of course, I wanted to meet her. I would get to work writing her back right away.

"Are you okay, dear?" I heard a voice from across the curtains: Norma. I must have been crying harder than I thought.

"Yes, I'm fine. These are happy tears," I said loud enough for her to hear. "My daughter wrote me a letter. I haven't heard from her in several years."

"That's wonderful," Norma said. "Make sure you don't lose that connection. Life is too short."

"You're right about that," I said, thinking of Larry and Anna.

I pressed my call light, hoping that one of the aides could bring me some stationary or notebook paper so that I could get to work writing back to Linda right away. Luckily, the aide that arrived was in nursing school and had some extra notebook paper that she was willing to give me.

"Thank you so much," I said. "I really appreciate it."

"No problem," she replied.

Dearest Linda,

I love knowing your name, by the way. I'm so sorry to hear about your parents. That must have been incredibly difficult for you to go through. I'm also sorry to hear about your divorce. Sometimes things happen in life that we don't expect and they knock us down to our knees, but we always stand back up. I'm glad you have your dogs for comfort and relationship.

I would love to see you for a visit here at Pine Meadows. I'm awfully sorry that I am stuck here and can't meet with you in Oklahoma City at your convenience. But if you're willing to come to Michigan, I would love that. There is a Holiday Inn just down the street, or better yet, you could stay at my house and save some money during your trip. My house hasn't been sold yet, as I'm hoping to move back there as soon as I gain the strength.

I'm so happy to hear that you had a good childhood. That's what Larry and I wanted for you, a happy home, a stable environment, and a good childhood. At sixteen, we just weren't sure we were able to provide that. Hopefully when you come for your visit, we can talk some of these things through a bit more.

I'm so excited to see you, and likewise, am looking forward to seeing if you look like me. Until we connect again.

With Love,

Judith March

I took the letter to the activities department later that day on my way to dinner and asked Kathy to mail it out to the same address in Oklahoma City. She said that she would, with a smile on her face. I could tell she was happy to be a part of my newfound connection with my daughter.

At dinner, I told Denise and Ila about the letter from Linda and the one I wrote back.

"That's great news!" Denise said.

"And it's all thanks to you," I said.

"And the activities department," she said.

"Praise the Lord," Ila said. "He's really making things happen for you, Judith."

"I know. I'm really excited. Linda says she's willing to come here for a visit from Oklahoma City. I told her she could stay at the house while she's here," I said.

"Have you told her about Carolyn and Cindy? Or better yet, have you told Carolyn and Cindy about her? If she's going to be staying at your house, you're going to have to do that," Denise said.

I hadn't thought about that. I figured I'd just introduce them after Linda got here. But Denise was right. I'd have to tell them about each other beforehand.

"No, I haven't, but you've got a good point. I need to do that. I just don't know how," I said. "You know how Carolyn is. She'll have a fit."

"It's the right thing to do," Ila said.

"You might as well just do it, like ripping off a band-aid Tell Carolyn and Cindy first. Then tell Linda," Denise said.

"I suppose you're right," I said. I didn't have much of an appetite after this conversation.

A couple of days later Carolyn and Cindy came for a visit to Pine Meadows just to see how I was doing. Carolyn said she wanted to talk with the nurse about how my new medication had been working out. When she was finished, both she and Cindy came to my room just to chat and visit.

"The nurse says your medicine seems to be helping mom. They haven't noticed as many episodes of forgetfulness as before, so that's good," Carolyn said.

"I don't think I really had that many to begin with, but that's good news," I said.

"It's great news, Mom," Cindy said.

"I was able to climb the stairs in therapy the other day without help," I said. "Rob was right there with me just in case, but I walked up and down the six-inch steps by myself with no help."

"That's good to hear," Carolyn said. "How many steps were there?"

"There were only three, but he said we're going to start practicing doing it multiple times to simulate a flight of stairs like at home," I said.

I was stalling on the subject of Linda and I knew it. The girls would only be staying for long. I needed to get to the topic, and fast. Denise's voice kept ringing through my head: like ripping off a band-aid.

"Listen, girls, there's something pretty important I want to discuss with you today. It has to do with the past and something that happened between your father and me. Maybe we should have told you sooner, maybe not. But I'm going to tell you now and I don't want you to be upset. I want you to support me, because this is something that means a lot to me, okay?"

"Sure, Mom," Cindy said.

Carolyn didn't say anything.

"You know your father and I have been together a long time, since we were teenagers. He was truly the love of my life. Well, when we were sixteen, I got pregnant." I continued to hear Denise's words: like ripping off a band-aid.

Cindy gasped.

Carolyn still did not say anything.

"Our parents were pretty upset about the whole ordeal and wanted to send me away for the entire pregnancy. But your father and I agreed that we would give the baby up for adoption. We met with an adoption agency who assigned us to a couple, who we didn't know at the time, that would end up adopting our baby," I continued, with tears in my eyes.

Carolyn and Cindy both continued to remain silent, which was rare for them, especially for Carolyn.

"When I had the baby, she was a baby girl, born in 1958. The lock box that you found the other day, that was all I had of her. It includes a onesie that she wore in the hospital, her identification bracelet that says 'baby girl March', and a lock of her dark brown hair."

"So somewhere out there, we have a sister," Cindy said with a pensive tone.

"What do you mean, 'that was all that you had of her?' Do you have more now?" Carolyn asked, looking up with hunched shoulders.

She was always picking up on those kinds of things.

"As a matter of fact, I do. You see, they had us write letters to a family member we hadn't seen recently in activities a while back. I chose to write a letter to your older sister. I knew it was a long shot, as I didn't even know her name or where she was living, but the staff here was very kind and said they would help me as best they could. And Denise said her daughter worked in the family court system and she'd be willing to help as well. So, I wrote the letter, just explaining who I was and telling her that I was hopeful we could meet someday."

"Oh, Mom, this is so much to take in," Cindy said.

"I'm sorry, girls, but I really feel you deserve to know the truth. And I'm sorry I didn't tell you sooner. It's just that your father was pretty close-minded about it. He never wanted to discuss it, let alone with you girls. I think it just broke his heart too much," I said.

"So, did they deliver the letter?" Carolyn asked.

"Between the activities department and Denise's daughter, I was able to find out that your older sister's name is Linda Grime. Her parents' names were Rick and Sonya Grime, but they have since passed away. We were able to get an address to deliver the letter and Linda and I have been corresponding back and forth a few times. She is making plans to come visit here soon," I said.

"Have you told her about us?" Cindy asked.

"Not yet. I wanted to tell you about her first," I said.

"Thank you for that," Carolyn said.

"Where does she live?" Cindy asked.

"She lives in Oklahoma City," I answered.

"Oh my, and she's coming for a visit here? Where is she going to stay?" Cindy asked.

"At the house," I said.

"At the house?" Carolyn exclaimed. "We can't just let some stranger stay at the house!"

"She's not a stranger Carolyn. She's my daughter and your sister."

"Mother, you're not thinking straight. You don't even know this woman. There's a Holiday Inn right down the street that would be just fine. I'll even foot the bill," Carolyn said.

"She's staying at the house and that's final. It's my house," I said.

"I hope you know what you're doing mother," Carolyn said right before she and Cindy left. Neither one seemed to be all that thrilled about the news.

Chapter 20

It wasn't long until I received another letter from Linda Grime, stating that she was finalizing her plans to come for a visit!

Dear Judith,

I hope this letter finds you well and enjoying the warm weather that has hopefully finally hit Michigan. I'm writing today to set up a visit with you, if you would still like to do so. I'm not sure if I mentioned in prior letters, but I am a retired teacher, so I have plenty of flexibility in my schedule to set up a time. I was thinking maybe the first week of July, unless you have other plans for the Fourth of July, we could spend the holiday together. If your offer still stands to allow me to stay at your home, perhaps we could possibly have a cookout?

As you can see, I am anticipating our visit and have already been planning it in my head. However, if you have other plans, feel free to knock me down a peg! I'm just so excited to finally meet you. One thing I haven't asked, do you have any other children? Will I be meeting them too? I'd be excited to know if I have siblings, being an only child my entire life. I apologize if this question is too personal.

How do you like it there at Pine Meadows? Do they treat you well? I looked up the facility online. It looks nice. You mentioned in an earlier letter about going back home soon. Are you any closer to returning home?

I'm sorry for seeming nosy, I just want to get to know as much about you as I can!

With Love,

Linda Grime

I found her letter charming, and couldn't wait to respond. Luckily, the activities department had stocked me up with stationary, knowing that I'd be writing several letters in the next few weeks.

Dear Linda,

Your letter was just wonderful and came at the most opportune time. Yes, the first week of July sounds perfect for a visit. I would be happy for you to stay at the house and will make sure you have the address for your travels. I am looking forward to our Fourth of July cookout!

I'm so proud of you for being a teacher. What grades and what subjects did you teach? When did you retire? It takes a strong-willed person to be a teacher, and they certainly don't get enough credit.

One thing I haven't mentioned in my letters, that I probably should have, is that I do have two other daughters, Carolyn and Cindy. They are both younger than you, of course, but they are both Larry's and my daughters as well, your full-blooded sisters. Carolyn is older and Cindy is the youngest. I did tell them about you the other day and that you would be coming for a visit soon. ~~Neither of them is upset or angry, so I don't want you to be worried that there will be any hard feelings~~*.*

Pine Meadows is an okay place. It was quite an adjustment when I first arrived here. I certainly would rather be home. The thing is, Carolyn is my Power of Attorney and it's up to her if I return home or not. I'm doing therapy here to get stronger, and it's helping, plus I'm on some new medication that the staff says is working wonders for me, so I'm hoping Carolyn will let me give it a try at home here soon. She wants someone staying with me all the time, however, and hasn't been able to find anyone who can stay with me at night. I'm holding out hope that we find someone soon. I do have some good friends here at Pine Meadows, though, that I would miss

dearly.

I'm very much looking forward to seeing you in July. I will be counting down the days. It's actually not that far away! See you soon.

With Love,

Judith March

Later that day, at lunch, I told the ladies about my upcoming visit with Linda Grime.

"She's coming for a visit the first week of July," I said.

"That's wonderful, Judith!" Denise said.

"I'm both nervous and excited," I admitted. "I'm excited to meet her and spend time with her, but I'm nervous that Carolyn and Cindy won't take a liking to her."

"Something to pray about," Ila said.

"How did they react when you told them about Linda?" Denise asked.

"Odd," I replied. "They really didn't say much. Well, Carolyn didn't say much, other than I shouldn't let Linda stay at the house when she comes for her visit. And you know how Cindy just follows Carolyn's lead."

"You're letting Linda stay at your house while she's here for her visit?" Denise asked.

"Yes," I said.

"I'm not so sure that's a good idea either," she said.

"Why?" I asked. "She's my daughter."

"But you barely know her," Denise said. "You don't know what she's truly capable of. Some of your valuables could come up missing."

"I don't think she's capable of that," I said. "I trust her."

"Based on a few letters?"

"Based on the fact that I gave birth to her!" I said a little louder than necessary, as others in the dining room looked over.

"Okay, okay," Ila said. "I don't think it's a big deal to let her stay at your house."

"Thank you, Ila," I said.

"But what are you going to do about all the items you said you and your daughters are trying to declutter?" Ila asked.

"That's a good question. We've got our work cut out for us between now and then."

A couple of days later, Carolyn and Cindy arrived to take me home for a visit. When we arrived home, there were still piles of clothes and other items lying around waiting to be sorted through.

"Girls, we have got a lot of work to do. We need to get this done by the first of July," I said.

"What? Why, mom?" Carolyn asked.

"Because Linda, your sister, is coming for her visit that week and she's going to be staying here. I don't want the place looking like a pigsty," I said.

"She's coming for a visit already?" Carolyn asked.

"Yes, and I, for one, am looking forward to it," I said. "And I want this house cleaned up before she gets here, so we need to sort out all these piles quickly."

"Did you even tell her about my offer to pay for the Holiday Inn? Carolyn asked.

"She's staying at the house Carolyn."

Carolyn sighed and I noticed that she rolled her eyes. I hoped that she changed her attitude toward Linda by the first of July

"We better get to work on these piles instead of bickering about this any longer," I said.

We worked all day sorting and organizing as much as we could. At the end of the day, we had five garbage bags full of things to throw away, ten boxes to go to recycling, and few items set aside to keep and put back away in the house. Carolyn and Cindy took the items back upstairs that were in the keep piles and put them back in their respective places and I returned the items to where they belonged downstairs.

At the end of the day, we were all exhausted. I needed a nap on the couch before returning to Pine Meadows, but it was getting to be dinnertime. When I woke up, Cindy suggested ordering a pizza before taking me back, which the three of us agreed was a great idea. Carolyn ordered for delivery and we all sat around the dining room table eating our pepperoni stuffed-crust pizza like we hadn't eaten in days. I realized then how much of a shock it must have been for the two of them to find out that they had an older sister that they never knew about. I had known the entire time, but they didn't. It really hadn't been fair. I needed to cut them some slack.

When we returned to Pine Meadows, as usual, Carolyn checked me back in, and Cindy walked with me back to my room. Then Carolyn arrived at my room so they could both tell me goodbye. It was usually a pretty quick goodbye, but this time I wanted to make sure to let them know how much they meant to me and that it wasn't just Linda Grime that I was focused on.

"I want you girls to know how much I love you both," I said.

"I love you too, Mom," Cindy said.

"I love you, too," Carolyn added.

"I appreciate you both very much for all that you've done for me. I'm not just talking about today, although I do appreciate everything we did today. I appreciate you both remaining so close with your old mother."

"Of course, Mom," Cindy said.

"We just want what's best for you, Mother," Carolyn added.

"I know," I said. "I want what's best for all of us."

The next day was a beautiful day, and after lunch, Pat asked me to sit outside with him for a while. I agreed without hesitation and we made our way out to the front patio with the assistance of our aides.

We chatted about a few other topics until inevitably Pat asked me how the search was going for Linda. I told him how things had progressed and that we had gotten to the point that Linda was going to come for a visit the first week of July.

"That's wonderful!" he said, with a big smile on his face, "She'll be here for the Fourth of July!"

"Yes," I said. "I think she wants to host a cookout at my house that day."

"At your house?" Pat asked.

"Yes, at my house, she's going to stay there during her visit," I said.

"Are you sure that's a good idea?" Pat asked gently.

"I don't know why people keep asking me that," I said. "She's my daughter. I know I haven't seen her for sixty years, but I gave birth to her. What's the worst that can happen if she stays in my home for a few days?"

Pat laughed, "You're right. I guess the rest of us just see her as a stranger, but it's true, she is your daughter. You have every right to let her stay in your home. I'm sorry."

"It's okay," I said. "Thank you for understanding. You're a good friend, Pat."

"You're a good friend too, Judith, I just don't want to see you get hurt."

"I won't get hurt," I said. "I promise."

Chapter 21

Linda and I sent a few other letters before the first week of July just to confirm her visit and to wrap up the details. I treasured every letter, folded each one, and put it in the lock box. Linda's final letter stated that she would be arriving on June thirtieth and would come straight to Pine Meadows before going to the house to drop off her things. I felt this would be the perfect time for her to meet Carolyn and Cindy as well, and then have Carolyn and Cindy check me out of Pine Meadows so we could all show her the house.

When I told Carolyn and Cindy the plan, they both agreed on the condition that if anything felt out of sorts one of them would spend the night at the house as well. I felt that was a bit extreme, and possibly offensive to Linda, but reluctantly agreed.

June thirtieth came and I was just a nervous wreck. Carolyn and Cindy arrived at Pine Meadows first, around one o'clock. We visited for a while. And then a woman arrived at my door who looked like an older version of Cindy. She had long, dark, graying hair with a swarthy skin tone and large brown eyes the shape of chestnuts, just like Larry's. She smiled and asked if I was Judith March. I said I was.

"My name is Linda Grime," she said.

"Oh!" was all I could say before I got up from my chair and gave her a hug. I forgot all about the rule regarding calling for someone to help before getting up. I just wanted to hug my baby girl.

She hugged me back and we both cried for a long while.

After we released the hug, Carolyn and Cindy made room for her to sit on the bed and I went back to sit in my chair.

"Linda, these are my other daughters, Carolyn and Cindy. Carolyn and Cindy, this is Linda," I said. I wasn't quite sure how else to make their introductions.

"It's nice to meet you," Carolyn said.

"Yes, it's nice to meet you," Cindy said.

"It's nice to meet you both," Linda said. "I've never had siblings before. This is so exciting for me," she added with a smile.

Cindy smiled, "So you grew up as an only child?"

"Yes, not that it was bad. But I always wondered what it would be like to have sisters," Linda said.

"And now you do!" I said. "What do you say we all head back to the house for now? Pine Meadows will still be here in the morning."

"Good idea," Carolyn said.

As we made our way back to the house, I prayed everything would go okay and that Carolyn and Cindy wouldn't feel the need to spend the night with Linda and make her feel uncomfortable. So far, things seemed to be going well. I was keeping my fingers crossed that they would stay that way.

"Oh, what a beautiful home," Linda said as we walked in the front door.

"I apologize, we're in the process of sorting and re-organizing, so there are some items out of place here and there," I said. "You'll just have to excuse the mess."

"Oh, there's no mess at all, don't worry about it, just show me the kitchen and the nearest grocery store and I'll be fine," Linda laughed.

Carolyn, Cindy, and I laughed with her.

"I can show you the kitchen and the rest of the downstairs, but I'm afraid Carolyn and Cindy will have to show you to your sleeping arrangements upstairs. I can't quite tackle all the steps on my own yet. I can do a few, but not all of them," I said.

"It's no problem Judith. I'll come to your therapy sessions and cheer you on this week. We'll get you tackling those stairs," Linda said.

I smiled. No one had ever come to cheer me on in therapy before.

After the girls returned from upstairs, it was getting late and time to get back to Pine Meadows. I was hesitant as to whether or not Carolyn or Cindy was planning to stay with Linda. Neither one had given any indication.

Finally, the time came for Carolyn and Cindy to take me back to Pine Meadows.

"Are you sure you're going to be okay here on your own Linda? Cindy or I would be happy to stay here with you if you'd feel more comfortable," Carolyn offered.

"Thank you so much for the offer. That's very sweet of you, but I know you've got families of your own. And I'll be okay, I'm sure. The only thing I miss is my dogs, but they're fine at the kennel. I'm going to find the nearest grocery store and be fine," Linda said.

"I'm sorry we didn't think to stock groceries," Cindy said, with her head hung. "Things have been kind of hectic around here."

"It's quite alright," Linda said. "I'm kind of a picky eater anyway, so no worries!"

I felt bad also that the girls and I hadn't thought to stock the kitchen with groceries for Linda. But I also felt an overwhelming sense of relief that Carolyn wasn't going to spend the night with her.

When Carolyn and Cindy took me back to Pine Meadows that night, all I could feel was contentment about how the evening went and optimistic about how the upcoming week was going to play out.

The next day, Linda arrived to spend the day with me at Pine Meadows. She said whatever I usually did, that's what I should do, and she would just tag along. At lunchtime, she brought a protein shake while I ate with Ila and Denise. I couldn't wait to introduce her, however.

"Linda, these are my friends, Ila and Denise."

"Ila and Denise, this is Linda that I've been telling you so much about.

"It's nice to meet you," they said to each other.

"Denise's daughter is the one who helped me find you," I said to Linda. "If it hadn't been for her, we would have never made our connection."

"Oh my, thank you so much," Linda said to Denise.

"And Ila's been praying for us to meet since the day she found out about you," I said.

Both Ila and Linda smiled.

At two o'clock that day was activities. This day's activity was a card game again, and it was Skip-Bo. I sat with Pat since I still wasn't the greatest at Skip-Bo, and Linda sat with us, but didn't play. I introduced the two of them as I had made many introductions previously.

"It's nice to meet you, Linda," Pat said.

"Likewise," Linda said.

As Pat continued to assist me throughout the card game, I explained to Linda the story of how it was the activities department that initiated my writing a letter to her. I told her how Kathy from the activities department had initially tried to find her address and had some success before

I turned to Denise's daughter for the remainder of the search. I explained to her that although I wasn't a big fan of Pine Meadows overall and didn't want to live there permanently, I would never be able to repay them for what they had done for me, bringing her into my life.

After activities, we had some time together alone back in my room for a while. Today wasn't a therapy day for me, although I wished it had been so Linda could see how good I was doing. She said she would cheer me on tomorrow.

"So, tell me about Pat," she said with a wink.

"There's nothing to tell," I said, laughing. "He's just a friend."

"He really dotes on you, Judith."

"He's a kind man," I said.

"Are you sure that's all?"

"I'm sure. Larry just passed away a couple of months ago. I'm not interested in seeing anyone else so soon. Pat knows that. He knows we are just friends. Although we were king and queen of the prom a while back," I laughed.

"Ooooh, king and queen of the prom. That's going places," Linda smiled.

"But seriously, we're close friends, like Ila and Denise, he just happens to be a man," I said.

"Okay, how's the food here?" she asked. "I wouldn't be able to stand it if the food was bad."

"It's not terrible," I said. "I've had worse."

"But you're telling me it's not great?" she asked.

"Basically," I said.

"What I really want to know is, how does the staff treat you here?" she asked.

"It depends on the day and time and the staff member," I said. "Some of them are really good and do a great job, but then some just can't because they're understaffed and they don't have time to answer our call lights on time. Some of them are just here for the paycheck and you can tell, because they're gruff and rough. Some of them are smart-mouthed little know-it-alls who deserve a kick in the pants if you know what I mean. Occasionally, it'll be my lucky day and I'll find a rose between the thorns."

"But they don't ever abuse you here, right?" Linda asked.

"Oh, heavens no," I said. "They might make me wait up until the last second of almost wetting myself, I might get a cold cup of coffee if I ask for one mid-morning, or I might have to wait forty-five minutes to get ready for the day, but that's about it. Why do you ask?"

"Well, I've just been thinking, I know you don't want to live here. And I don't want you to have to live here either. This might be a little too soon, but I thought maybe I might have a solution for that. Why don't you come live with me?"

Chapter 22

"Go live with you?" I asked, in shock.

"Yes, with me. I'm home all day. I'd be willing to be your caregiver. Then you wouldn't have to live in a place like this anymore, waiting on aides to answer your call light."

"In Oklahoma City?" I asked.

"Yes. I realize it would be a bit of an adjustment, but I think you'd be happier," Linda said.

I couldn't believe what I was hearing. *I never would have dreamed that she would make such an offer. It was so tempting. But like so many of my friends and family had already pointed out, even though she was my daughter, I barely knew her. Could I really pack up and move in with her?*

"What about Carolyn and Cindy?" I asked.

"Well they would be able to come visit any time, or you could come back and visit them at any time, either way," Linda assured.

I was used to seeing the girls almost every day. I wasn't sure it would work to have an occasional visit.

"That's exceptionally nice of you to offer Linda. Could I think about it for a while?" I asked. "As much as I want to get out of Pine Meadows, I'm not sure I can give up my entire life here in Bedford Hills."

"I understand," she said. "Just know that my offer always stands."

The following day, Linda tagged along for my therapy session, as promised. Rob was my therapist again, and he put me through the usual paces in the parallel bars.

"Do you usually work this hard or are you just showing off?" Linda asked me as she laughed good-naturedly.

"She usually works this hard," Rob answered seriously. "She wants to go home."

"Oh, believe me, I know," Linda said.

After my workout, we headed to the stairs, the six-inch steps, and, with Rob standing behind me, I walked up all three steps with ease. I smiled as I got to the platform, turned, and made my way back down.

"Let's try that two more times," Rob said.

I looked at him with wide eyes.

"You want to simulate a flight of steps like you have at home," Rob said.

"You're right," I said.

So, I turned around and faced the steps again. With Rob behind me, I started up the steps again and made my way to the top. It was a bit more of a struggle this time, but I didn't want to admit anything. I turned around and made my way back down. Then, I turned around for the final time and placed my foot up onto the step, I hoisted myself up onto the step, but it took a noticeable effort, and the same with the next two. Rob had to have his hand on my gait belt. I felt ashamed that I couldn't do the third round of steps on my own.

"You'll get there," Rob said. "It won't be long."

"I don't have any stairs in my home," Linda whispered in my ear.

"We'll get it next time," I told Rob.

Linda said she wasn't going be able to make it to Pine Meadows until after breakfast, which I found myself a bit thankful for. Then I felt guilty. I wanted to spend every minute of every day with her while she was here, but I also wanted to tell Ila and Denise about her offer to let me come stay with her in Oklahoma City and see what they thought about it, and I couldn't

do that with Linda here.

So, at breakfast, I sat down with Ila and Denise to get their opinion.

"How is your visit going with Linda?" Ila asked.

"It's going great, thank you for asking," I said. "She's a wonderful woman. I'm learning

so much about her."

"That's great!" Denise said.

"There's just one thing I'm not sure about," I said.

"What's that?" Denise asked.

"She wants me to go live with her in Oklahoma City!" I said.

"What?!" Denise asked.

"Oh, Judith, I'm not so sure that's a good idea," Ila said.

That's when I knew I wasn't wrong for hesitating about answering Linda. Ila hardly ever

spoke up.

"I know that's not a good idea," Denise said. "You hardly know her. I know she's your

daughter and everything, but you can't just leave your home here and your other two daughters."

"I know. I told Linda I needed time to think about it. I didn't give her an answer yet," I

said.

"Judith, you need to tell her 'thanks, but no thanks.' I mean, think of how Carolyn and

Cindy would feel if you just up and moved away." Denise said.

"I know, I've thought about that. Plus, I don't want to leave my home. But I do want to

leave here," I said quietly.

"But that's what you've been working toward. Don't give up hope. It can still happen," Denise said.

"Not unless Carolyn and Cindy can find someone who can stay with me at night. And yesterday I practiced walking up an entire flight of stairs. I barely made it," I said.

"There's always hope," Ila said. "And always prayer."

The Fourth of July arrived and it was time to spend time with all of the girls together in my home. I was looking forward to having them all together again and to having our cookout. Linda had gone to the grocery store and bought steaks and hamburgers to grill on Larry's gas grill, Carolyn brought potato salad and baked beans, and Cindy baked a cheesecake. I brought some table favors we had made in activities with small American flags and little chocolate candy bases.

Carolyn helped Linda out at the grill and Cindy and I spent time together decorating the dining room and setting the table. We would have eaten outside, but it was a sweltering ninety-five degrees and sunny out, and Cindy can't tolerate that temperature for too long.

While we were decorating, Cindy and I had a rare opportunity to have a one-on-one chat about how things had been going lately.

"What do you think about Linda, honey?" I asked.

"She seems nice," Cindy said. "I haven't been around her too much to form an opinion yet."

"Yeah," I said. "She's been spending most of her time at Pine Meadows. She's a great person. I think you girls will really like her once you get to know her."

"I'm sure," Cindy said with a smile. "How is Pine Meadows?"

"It's about the same. I still want to leave, Cin. I still want to live here," I said.

"I understand. You know it's up to Carolyn-"

"I know. How are Brian and the boys?"

"They're doing well, Mom. Brian's job is keeping him busy. The boys are enjoying summer break. Derek has a summer job at the local car wash," Cindy said of her family.

"That's great," I said. "Tell them I miss them. I hope to see them soon."

"They would have come today, but you know boys, always off with their friends. And Brian had to work," she said.

"I understand," I said.

Carolyn and Linda entered then with the steak and hamburgers from the grill and placed them in the center of the dining room table. Both were smiling and laughing as if they'd been joking around with each other outside. I took this as a good sign.

We all sat down together to eat as Carolyn said the blessing.

"Be present at our table Lord

Be here and everywhere adored

Thy people bless and grant that we

May feast in paradise with thee.

Amen."

As we all ate dinner, I couldn't help but feel full of love. Everyone was laughing, smiling, and getting along great. The day was just perfect. I decided not to bring up Linda's offer to Carolyn or Cindy just yet. I didn't want to spoil the day.

Linda told stories of her days as a teacher. She said she used to teach third grade. She had a lot of interesting tales about teaching young ones, both serious and humorous. She told us about moving to Oklahoma City because of her ex-husband's job as a railway worker and of how much she didn't want to leave El Paso when she did. She said she'd since adjusted to Oklahoma City, but will always hold a grudge against her ex-husband for making her move away from the home she knew and loved.

"Why don't you move back now?" Carolyn asked.

"Both of my parents have passed away," Linda said. "I don't have any ties there anymore. For the past forty years, I've built my life in Oklahoma City, even though I didn't want to, so I might as well stay."

Carolyn talked about her life as an accountant and said that she'd been pretty busy throughout the first part of the year, but that this was her slow time.

"I can help Mom get more done around the house right now to get it prepared for whatever may happen," she said.

"Do you have any family?" Linda asked.

"Yes, I have a husband and two daughters. My husband is away on a business trip right now or else he would be here with us. He works for a local law firm as an attorney. My daughters are both grown with families of their own," Carolyn said.

"That's wonderful," Linda said. "Are you a grandmother?"

"Yes, my daughter has a baby girl, named Olivia. She's two. My other daughter is married, but she doesn't have any children yet."

Linda turned to me, "So you're a great-grandmother!"

"Yes," I said proudly. I realized I hadn't shown her any pictures of my grandchildren yet. *How could I have forgotten?* "After lunch, we'll get the photo albums out, right Carolyn?"

"Of course, Mother"

By then, it was Cindy's turn to tell her story. She told Linda how she had been a stay-at-home mother all her life to her two boys who were still teenagers, and could still be a handful at times. Cindy explained where her family was for the day also and said that it was kind of nice to have a day off from being Mom.

"Wow, I give you a lot of credit for that," Linda said. "They say it takes a lot of work to raise a family full-time."

"It takes more work than people realize," Cindy said.

I could tell she was happy to have the validation, as she didn't get it very often from Carolyn.

After lunch, Cindy and I cleared the table while Linda and Carolyn boxed up the leftovers. Then, Cindy and Carolyn did the dishes, while Linda and I went through the photo albums.

First, I showed her photos of Larry when he was a child, then photos of me when I was young. Then I showed her the two of us together when we first started dating. We were only about fifteen. I didn't have any photos of me pregnant with her, but I did show her photos of around that time period, when Larry and I were sixteen. I also presented our wedding photos when we were twenty-four and then Carolyn's baby photos, and not long after, Cindy's baby photos. I showed her photos of the girls growing up throughout the years and their respective wedding photos and then the photos that were the most precious to me, other than the ones of Larry of course, my grandchildren. I showed her all four of them as newborns and then their growing up years. And finally, I showed her a picture of my great-granddaughter. We had recently printed her picture from Carolyn's iPhone at the local Walgreens for the album. She was a doll baby.

"What a beautiful baby girl," Linda said.

"I know," I said. "I just can't take my eyes off of her. She's another reason I want to come home so badly, you see?"

"Yes, I understand," Linda said.

I was trying to get Linda to understand that, while I appreciated her offer to go to Oklahoma City, I just couldn't leave my family here in Bedford Hills.

The rest of our day was wonderful: the girls all got to know each other better, and Linda and I got to know each other even more. We spent the day just talking and reminiscing. It wasn't long until it was time for me to return to Pine Meadows.

Carolyn and Cindy got up to get ready for the trip.

"I'll take her back," Linda said.

"Are you sure?" Carolyn asked.

"Of course. I know the way. I'd be happy to," Linda said.

"Okay, if you're sure," Carolyn said.

Carolyn hardly ever relented, but I could tell she was exhausted after such a long day. I wasn't surprised that she gave in this time.

So, Linda and I headed back to Pine Meadows. She checked me in for the evening and then came back to my room to say goodbye.

"You have such a beautiful family, Judith," she said.

"Oh, thank you," I said. "I hope someday you'll feel comfortable enough to feel like you're a part of it."

"Today was wonderful," she said. "But I can see why you'd hesitate in wanting to come live in Oklahoma City. Who would want to leave such a wonderful family and adorable grandchildren?"

"Well, that's just it, Linda, I don't want to hurt your feelings. And I do appreciate your offer, but I just don't think I can do it right now," I blurted out.

"It's okay, Judith, I understand. I was actually thinking of something else that might work. What if I moved here? Then you'd have someone to stay with you at night."

Chapter 23

"Moved here? As in, moved into the house? To be my full-time caregiver?" I asked. I was a bit shocked at her generous offer.

"Yes, Judith. I have no ties to Oklahoma City, as I shared earlier, well, other than my dogs of course. My only previous ties were my parents in El Paso and since they've passed away, my only family, as such, is all of you here in Bedford Hills. I'm retired, I don't have a job holding me back. I live in an apartment with a monthly lease. It'll all work out. You need a caregiver and I have the time and willingness to be one as long as you'll let the dogs come along."

"Oh my, this is all so much to take in. How generous of you," I said. "I mean, words can't express my gratitude. Of course, I'll have to talk it over with Carolyn, but I'm sure she'll be fine with it. We've been trying to find a nighttime caregiver for weeks now. She'll be thrilled to know that you've offered to take that on as well as the shifts that she and Cindy were going to have to cover."

Linda smiled. "It's my pleasure to be able to help you out, Judith."

"We'll have to get the three of you girls together tomorrow to discuss this so we can move forward as soon as possible. I don't want to stay at Pine Meadows any longer than I have to!" I said.

The next day, I asked Carolyn and Cindy to meet Linda and I at Pine Meadows for a discussion.

"What's this all about?" Carolyn asked.

I explained to her Linda's generous offer to move to Bedford Hills and move into the house to be my full-time caregiver so that I could move out of Pine Meadows and move back in at home.

"Did the two of you just come up with this scheme last night?" Carolyn asked. She did not sound thrilled about the idea at all.

"It was my idea," Linda said. "Like I told Judith, I don't have any ties to Oklahoma City. I'd be more than happy to come here and help out."

"I don't know about this …," Cindy's voice trailed off.

"Girls, this is wonderful. I can move back home now. Don't you see?" I said. I was getting exasperated with their reactions.

"Mother, this would mean having someone we've all just met move into our home," Carolyn said. "No offense Linda, we really like you, we just hardly know you yet."

"Carolyn!" I practically shouted. I couldn't believe she could be so rude. "She's been a guest in our home for several days—a very polite guest at that!"

"Mother, we're talking about someone moving in, living there, for good, not just a guest," Carolyn said.

"I'm sorry to have created a problem," Linda said. "I simply wanted to help. I know Judith doesn't like living here at Pine Meadows."

"Carolyn, we had an agreement. We agreed that I could go home when we found someone who could stay with me at night. Well, I've found someone. Now, you're backing out on our agreement?" I asked.

"Mother, that's not exactly the same. I never agreed to allow that person to move into our home," she said.

"Could Linda get an apartment somewhere in Bedford Hills and just spend the nights at the house?" Cindy asked.

"I wouldn't have that!" I said.

Carolyn sighed, "We'll have to work out the financial details of the deal later on, but I suppose we could give it a try." She looked at Cindy. "Mom and Linda seem set on the deal already and it would solve the problem of a night time caregiver. Okay, we'll give it a try on a trial basis."

Linda and I gave each other a high five and a cheer. I knew she would need some time to get her affairs in order in Oklahoma City, but I couldn't wait to leave Pine Meadows. Of course, I was going to have to tell my friends first. That was going to be the difficult part.

At dinner that night, I sat down next to Ila and Denise to tell them the news.

"I'm leaving," I said, trying not to smile too big.

"Where are you going?" Ila asked.

"I'm going home," I said. I told them about Linda's offer and Carolyn's initial reluctance, but then acceptance of Linda's offer to move into the house to be my caregiver.

"I can't believe she agreed to it," Denise said.

"What do you mean?" I asked.

"I can't believe Carolyn agreed to let Linda move into your house. You guys barely know her," Denise said.

"She's been staying there all week," I said. "And there's been no problem. She's my daughter just like Carolyn and Cindy. I would let either of them move in if they needed or wanted to."

Denise shook her head.

"She seems like a nice lady," Ila said.

"Thank you, Ila. I think she is a wonderful person, which is why I trust her completely to stay in my house currently and to move into my house in the future. I'll be living there with her, so I don't see what the fuss is about," I said.

"Is Carolyn going to pay her to be your caregiver? Or is she going to live rent-free in your house? Have you thought about these things, Judith? I'm sure Carolyn has," Denise asked.

To be honest, no, I hadn't thought about those things. I usually leave those things up to Carolyn, which is probably why she did get a little upset earlier. Sometimes I do forget that there's a lot on her plate.

"I'm sure Carolyn and Linda will work those details out amongst themselves," I said. "There's no need to get me involved."

"I'm happy for you that you get to go home, don't get me wrong, I just worry that maybe this arrangement isn't for the best," Denise said.

"What do you mean by that?" I asked defensively.

"Judith, we're older now and not in our best shape. You're lucky to have Carolyn, but she's not going to be around constantly. I'm afraid you might get taken advantage of by someone you don't know very well," she said.

"Taken advantage of, how?" I asked.

"In any way possible," she said. "It's 2020. Listen to the news. It happens all the time. I'm only telling you this because I care about you as a friend, you know?"

"I appreciate that Denise. I really do. But my Linda would never do something like that. I just know it. She's my daughter. I've gotten to know her over the past few days and I know she's not that type of person," I said.

"Well, in that case, I wish you the best of luck when the time comes," Denise said.

"Yes, good luck," said Ila.

A few days later, it was time for Linda to head back home to Oklahoma City. Carolyn, Cindy, Linda, and I all decided to have a meal at the house to say goodbye before Linda left. Carolyn prepared a ham, Cindy made twice-baked potatoes, pasta salad, and deviled eggs, and Linda made a triple-layered chocolate cake that looked divine.

As we all sat around the dining room table and ate, the atmosphere was a bit different than that of the Fourth of July. There wasn't as much chatter at first, until I finally decided to break the ice.

"How soon do you plan on coming back, Linda?" I asked.

"It'll take me about a month to wrap things up in Oklahoma City," she said.

I tried not to let my face fall. I was really hoping not to stay at Pine Meadows any longer than a couple of weeks, but I tried to be understanding.

"That will give us enough time to prepare things around here," Carolyn said.

"I suppose we'll need to exchange cell phone numbers," Linda said.

"Oh yes, good idea," Carolyn said.

They swapped phones across the table and exchanged numbers.

I got my cell phone out from my purse and handed it to Linda. "Will you put your number in my phone, too, please?" I asked.

"Of course!" she replied. She added her number to my phone and then my number to her own phone. "We'll be in contact daily," she promised.

It wasn't long until we had to clear the table and say goodbye to Linda since her flight would be leaving soon. I didn't want to say goodbye, but at least I knew she'd be returning fairly soon. Still, I had tears in my eyes when it came down to my turn to give her a hug goodbye.

"I'm going to miss you!" I said, as the tears in my eyes spilled down my cheeks.

"I'm going to miss you, too!" she said as she cried also. "But don't worry, I'll be back, and next time, for good! You won't be able to get rid of me."

"I hope not!" I said.

She smiled and gathered her bags and headed out the front door. I couldn't wait to see her walk back through it again.

A couple of days later, I got a chance to chat with Pat while we sat outside on the front patio of Pine Meadows on a nice sunny day. I realized I was going to miss this, and miss him. Hopefully Carolyn, or Linda, would bring me back for visits to see him and sit outside with him.

"I have some news," I said as we sat with our faces toward the sun.

"Oh yeah? What's that?" Pat asked, eyes closed.

"I'm going home in about a month."

"Oh?" he asked. I thought I detected a note of disappointment, but maybe I was only wanting to.

"Yes, you remember my daughter Linda, that I gave up for adoption?"

"Well, yes, of course," he said.

"She's moving to Bedford Hills, to my house, to be my caregiver full-time," I said.

"Wow, that's a big undertaking," he said. "Good for you though."

I expected him to be more excited for me, but for some reason, he was pretty subdued about the whole thing.

"I know. It's going to take her about a month to get her affairs in order in Oklahoma City, but then she will move here into my house and I'll move back home," I said. "I'll still come back here to visit though. I'll be sure of that."

Pat opened his eyes and smiled. "I'll look forward to your visits," he said.

"I just can't wait to be free from having to use the call button for everything I want to do, you know? I want my freedom back," I said.

"I can understand that," he said. "Are your other daughters going to be around to keep an eye on things?"

"Carolyn and Cindy? Oh, they wouldn't miss a beat," I said. "But why do you ask?"

"I just want to make sure you all are being careful," Pat said.

"Careful about Linda, you mean?" I asked.

"Well, just careful about the situation. You really just met her. I just don't want to see someone taking advantage of you, Judith."

Coming from anyone else, I would have gotten defensive. But he said it with such kindness that I had a hard time getting angry with him over his comment about my own daughter.

"I appreciate your concern. I really do. But there's nothing to worry about. Linda is my daughter. She stayed at the house for an entire week over the Fourth of July and there were no issues. We barely knew her then. We know her a lot better now and she's a part of our family. I have no problems letting her move into my home with me."

"As long as you're comfortable with it, that's all that matters," Pat smiled.

I smiled back. We faced the sunshine and enjoyed the warm rays on our faces.

Chapter 24

A month later, Linda moved to Bedford Hills from Oklahoma City and moved into the house with Rocco and Sadie. Once she got settled in, it was time to start packing my things up at Pine Meadows. Linda, Carolyn, and Cindy all arrived to help pack up what little I had been allowed to take to Pine Meadows when I first moved in.

As we began to pack, I started to wonder just exactly what we were packing everything up for.

"Carolyn, why are we packing up all of my things? Am I moving to a different room?" I asked.

Carolyn and Cindy exchanged glances.

"No, Mother, you're going home to live with Linda, remember?" Carolyn said.

"Oh yeah, that's right," I said, although I didn't remember. I was elated to be leaving Pine Meadows and to be going home, however.

As we finished packing, I started to wonder why Carolyn and Linda were taking my things out to the car.

"Cindy, why are we loading up all of my things? Am I moving to a different nursing home?" I asked. I was quite fearful at this point. I didn't want to leave.

"No Mother, you're going to go back home to live with Linda, remember?" Cindy said in her soft, reassuring tone.

"Oh yes, that's right," I said. I didn't remember, but I knew I could trust Cindy.

When Carolyn and Linda came back from loading the final items into the car, they asked if I would like to say goodbye to anyone before I left. I did say goodbye to my roommate Norma,

Denise and Ila who were in activities, and Pat who was sitting outside as usual. I told them all I would come back to visit frequently, and hoped that Linda would help me do that.

When we made our way back to the house, the girls helped me in and helped me get settled in the front room. Carolyn and Linda unloaded the bags from the car as Cindy sat with me in the front room.

"Is there anything I can get you, Mother? Do you want a cup of tea or anything?" she asked.

"No thank you. Are we going to organize items today? I don't see any piles to go through." I said.

"Nope, we're just going to enjoy having you home," she said.

I laughed, "Having me home?"

"Yes," she said. "Having you home from now on, with Linda."

Carolyn and Linda came in with the last of my belongings then and were trying to decide where to arrange everything when Cindy asked to meet with both of them in the kitchen. While the three of them were meeting in the kitchen, I stretched out on the sofa and took a nap. It had been a long day.

When I woke up, Carolyn, Cindy, and Linda were all arranging my items in the front room, speaking in hushed voices so as not to wake me. I cleared my throat so they'd know I was awake.

"Oh, Mother, you're awake, great," Carolyn said.

"Yes ..." I trailed off.

"Look, I think we're going to need to make another appointment with Dr. Stanbery," she said.

"Why?" I asked.

"I think he needs to adjust your memory medication," Carolyn replied.

"You think there's something wrong with my memory again?" I asked.

"I think we need to let the doctor take a look at you," she said.

I sighed, "Okay."

"I called while you were asleep and they have an appointment available tomorrow at two o'clock. Linda is going to take you," she said.

I sighed again. I'd still have to follow some rules even though I was home.

"Okay," I said.

The next morning, I woke from my makeshift bed on the sofa to all of my items spread out around me. I was so used to pressing a call button before moving, I almost reached for it before getting my clothes out for the day. The girls had unpacked my toiletries in the half bathroom downstairs, so I placed my clothes in the basket of my walker and headed toward the bathroom.

I got myself ready for the day and got dressed, all without difficulty. When I was finished, I made my way out of the bathroom to find Linda in the kitchen making breakfast. I asked if I could help, but of course she insisted that I sit down and relax.

I sat down at the kitchen table to where she served fresh brewed coffee, home-made waffles, scrambled eggs, bacon, and bananas and oranges. It was the best breakfast I'd had in a long time.

Later that afternoon, at two o'clock, was my appointment with Dr. Stanbery. Linda drove me to the appointment and we met with the doctor regarding my memory issues.

"What seems to be going on here lately, Judith?" Dr. Stanbery asked.

"I don't really think there is much of a problem doctor," I said. "I guess Cindy was worried about some things I said last night, but I don't think I have an issue."

"Has anyone else noticed anything out of the ordinary?" Dr. Stanbery asked, looking at Linda.

"Doctor, I'll be honest, I haven't noticed a thing. She seems perfectly fine to me. She got herself up, got dressed and ready for the day today without help, came out and ate breakfast. She didn't say anything off at all," Linda said.

Dr. Stanbery put me through the same test as before, with the three words to remember, spelling world backward, and counting backward from one hundred by sevens. This time I passed it with flying colors.

"Judith, I'm impressed!" he said. "The medication we've put you on must be working wonders."

I didn't know what medication he was talking about, but I knew well enough to keep my mouth shut.

"That's great, Judith!" Linda said.

"I don't think we need to make any changes right now, but tell Carolyn to give me a call any time if need be, okay?" Dr. Stanbery said.

"Of course," I said.

"Actually, not to butt in Dr. Stanbery, but my name is Linda Grime, and I'm going to be Judith's primary caregiver from now on. I understand that Carolyn is her Power of Attorney, but if there are any concerns regarding her healthcare, I'd like to be involved also," Linda said.

"Ah, that is up to Judith and her family," Dr. Stanbery said.

"It's fine with me," I said.

"It has to be okay with Carolyn, too, Judith," Dr. Stanbery said. "It's the law."

"I understand," Linda said.

Later that evening, Carolyn and Cindy came over to the house for a visit.

"How did the appointment go?" Carolyn asked.

"What appointment?" I asked.

"Your doctor's appointment," she said.

"Oh yeah," I said. I didn't want to say much, because I forgot I went to the doctor. I looked to Linda for help.

"It went really well," she said. "Dr. Stanbery said her medicine must be working great, because she aced his memory test."

"Really?" Cindy asked.

"Yes," Linda said. "She did great."

"So, he didn't change any of her medication or increase the dosage?" Carolyn asked.

"No. He said if you had any questions or concerns you could call him, but as for right now, she's healthy," Linda said.

"I'll be calling him in the morning," Carolyn said.

That night, after Carolyn and Cindy left, I started getting ready for bed downstairs. I picked out my nightclothes and headed to the half bath to do my night routine. When I was finished, I headed upstairs and went to bed. It felt good to sleep in Larry's and my bed again, but oh, I missed him so much. It was the first time I'd slept in our bed without him since his last business trip over twenty-some years ago. I reached over to his side of the bed and just let the tears fall.

The next morning, I woke to Linda yelling, "Judith! Judith!"

"Yes!" I called out.

She came running up the stairs.

"What are you doing up here?" she asked.

"Sleeping," I replied.

"You're supposed to be sleeping on the sofa for now!" she exclaimed. "I thought something happened to you!"

"I'm sorry, I just wanted to sleep in my own bed," I said.

"If you want to go up the stairs, you have to have someone with you," she said. "Remember what the therapist said?"

I didn't remember what the therapist said, but apparently, he must have told us that.

"Okay, Okay, I won't go up the stairs without you anymore," I said.

The following day, Carolyn and Cindy came over for a visit and for dinner. Carolyn picked up a catered meal from one of the local restaurants so that no one would have to cook and we all sat down for a nice meal.

"Where's the centerpiece?" Carolyn asked.

"The what?" Linda asked.

"The centerpiece? We have a centerpiece in the middle of the dining room table, a glass dove, it's always here. Where is it?" Carolyn asked again.

"I don't remember seeing such a thing," Linda said.

"It's always been there," Cindy said.

"Remember, Mom?" Carolyn asked.

"Yes Carolyn, I remember. Your Aunt Rebecca gave it to your father and I for our twenty-fifth wedding anniversary present."

"We didn't box it up on accident, did we?" Cindy asked.

"Oh, I hope not!" I said.

"Don't worry, Mom, we'll find it," Carolyn said. "Let's eat."

As we ate our meal, I became the topic of conversation.

"So, let's be honest, Linda, how are things going with Mom in the house?"

"Well, we've had a couple of minor issues, but nothing too major that we couldn't handle, right, Judith?"

"I suppose so," I said, not knowing what she was talking about.

"Do you care to elaborate?" Carolyn asked.

"Oh, I found Judith upstairs this morning, unbeknownst to me, she had made her way up to the master bedroom and slept in her old bed last night. But we had a discussion about the importance of making sure someone is with her any time she attempts to go up or down those steps," Linda said.

Carolyn gasped, "Mom went up the stairs by herself?"

Linda gave a sheepish grin. "I was slightly impressed myself, but also firm in my direction to her to not ever do it again without help."

"Mom, you know that Linda's right, don't you?"

"Yes, I know, always ask for help. This place is no different than Pine Meadows," I said.

"That's a little extreme," Carolyn said.

"Other than that, things have been going great with Judith," Linda said. "We've been having a great time."

"Okay, please keep us informed of any other issues that come about," Carolyn said.

"I certainly will," Linda said.

As dinner ended, I felt more and more like a child and less like the matriarch of the family. They certainly weren't treating me like the head of the household. I wondered if things would ever go back to feeling the way they used to.

Chapter 25

Finally, the day came when I got up the nerve to ask Linda if I could move my things upstairs to my own bedroom.

"I know it will be more of a hassle for you to have to walk up and down the stairs with me, but I'd really like to sleep in my own room, rather than on the sofa, if you know what I mean," I pleaded.

"I understand Judith," she said. "Sure, let's make it work."

So, we moved all of my items upstairs to my bedroom, organized them, and put them away where they belonged. Linda helped me put clean sheets on the bed. And we dusted around all of my decorations that I had on display throughout the room, collected throughout the years.

Once we got everything all arranged and taken care of in the master bedroom, I was ready for a nap. I lay down on the bed and slept for a couple of hours. It felt good to finally sleep in Larry's and my bed again, with permission this time. This is what I'd been dreaming of ever since moving in to Pine Meadows.

When I woke up, I found that the aerial photo of our property that sat on the nightstand by the bed was missing. I could have sworn it was there when I went to sleep, but maybe it wasn't. Maybe it got lost in the shuffle of my move to Pine Meadows. But I was hoping we still had it somewhere, as it was important to Larry and me. I'd have to ask Carolyn next time I saw her. Maybe she just wrapped it up for safekeeping or something.

Now that I was awake, I wanted to go downstairs. I remembered I wasn't supposed to go down the steps without help, so I'd need to find Linda. We hadn't really worked out a plan yet for how I should call for her when I needed her, so this was tricky. I had no idea where she was. I looked in and around the rest of the rooms upstairs with no luck, so she had to be downstairs.

"Linda!" I hollered.

No answer.

"Linda!" I hollered a little louder.

Still no answer.

I looked out all of the windows of the second floor to see if she was outside. I didn't see any sign of her.

I was trapped on the second floor of my own home. *Well, at least I had a bathroom,* I thought.

I went to the top of the stairwell and tried a third time, "Linda!!"

"Yes, Judith?" she answered.

"Oh, thank goodness. I thought I'd be stuck up here all day. I'd like to come downstairs now, please," I said.

"Of course," she said, as she helped me down the steps with ease. She carried my walker and handed it to me when we reached the bottom.

"Thank you, dear."

"You're welcome."

"You know, I think we need to come up with some kind of system for me to be able to get hold of you," I said. "Something other than shouting, I don't like shouting."

"What do you suggest?" she asked. "I'm open to suggestions."

"Maybe a bell? Would that be okay?" I asked. I hoped that wasn't too demeaning.

"A bell? Well, I guess I can't think of anything else, so let's try it," she said.

"Okay," I said.

The following week, we implemented the bell system. I tried to use it sparingly and tried not to use it when she was within earshot and I could just call out her name. It seemed to be working pretty well, or at least I thought so. I didn't have to shout for her anymore if she was far away and she didn't have to worry about staying so close to me at all times.

Carolyn and Cindy came over around this time to help do some more sorting around the house and organizing as we still planned to donate a lot of items or throw things away just to get rid of clutter. We invited Linda to help with the process, but overall, Carolyn was the one who was always in charge of these get-togethers. This particular day, we were working in one of the spare bedrooms upstairs, Carolyn's old bedroom.

Carolyn said to donate all of the old clothes and shoes, although she was sure they were so outdated no one would ever want to wear them. She also said to donate her old record collection, even though I told her it was probably worth some money. She was on a donating spree when her face went blank.

"What's wrong, Carolyn?" Cindy asked.

"It's missing," she said.

"What's missing?" I asked.

"My old jewelry box. It's gone," Carolyn said.

"Oh, it's got to be here somewhere," I said.

"Let's keep looking," Cindy said.

So, we kept looking as we sorted, but the jewelry box didn't turn up. Carolyn was visibly upset.

"It had my class ring in it," she said with a frown.

"Are you sure you didn't take it to college with you?" Linda asked.

"I'm sure. It was right here," Carolyn said. Her face was red and her hands were trembling.

"We'll find it dear. It probably just got moved to a different room," I said.

"Yeah," Carolyn said, not sounding so convinced.

The following day, Linda and I decided to do some heavy cleaning in an effort to find some of these items that had been misplaced. We decided to start downstairs with a thorough dusting, vacuuming, and re-organizing of all the shelves. Linda's job was the vacuum, mine was to dust, and we were going to share the duty of re-organization.

I loathe dusting. It's my least favorite household chore, but it's one I can do with my walker, so I decided to take it. As I took down each knick-knack and dusted it as well as the space around it, I realized I own more knick-knacks than any one person should in a lifetime. The only items I was happy to dust were the framed pictures of my children and grandchildren. I was dusting away at them when I realized that the photo of my great-granddaughter was missing. *Why would the photo of my sweet Olivia be gone?* I had another photo of her in the photo album, but why would someone take the photo off the shelf? I was starting to worry that maybe we had an intruder.

I stopped what I was doing and walked out to the dining room where Linda was vacuuming and told her about Olivia's photo.

"I'm worried that someone's getting into the house," I said, my voice trembling.

"I wouldn't worry about that, Judith. We keep the doors locked all the time. I can get a security system set up, though, if you'd feel better," Linda said.

"Yes, that would make me feel better. And maybe things would stop going missing," I said.

"Okay, I'll call today and have them come set it up," she said.

"Thank you," I said with relief.

I went back to the front room to look for Olivia's picture.

A couple of days later, the security company arrived to set up and install the new home security system to protect the house. The whole thing looked complicated to me, but I was determined to figure it out because I did not want any more intruders coming into our home taking items that were precious to us. So, I followed along with the installers as they guided me step-by-step through the process and how the system worked. They installed sensors at the front, back, and side doors. At the front door, they placed a keypad where we would have to enter a code every time we came in or left. We'd also have to enter the code if the security system detected a threat and we were home and didn't note any threat, otherwise they would go ahead and call the police. The installers stated that police would arrive within five minutes of our alarm going off unless we typed in the code.

I felt much safer after the security system was in place and let the installers know that by trying to give them a plateful of fresh-baked chocolate chip cookies, but they said they weren't allowed to accept gifts. I would have given each one of them a hug, too, if I could, but I know that's not acceptable either. But at least Linda and I knew we didn't have to worry about items going missing.

The next morning, I woke up feeling pretty blah. I felt my forehead: no fever. I didn't feel sick, but something was off, like I was extraordinarily tired. I didn't feel like getting out of bed or getting myself ready for the day, so I rang my bell for Linda.

While waiting, I closed my eyes and drifted back to sleep for a moment. I don't normally sleep this late, but this morning was exceptional.

Linda woke me by nudging my shoulder, "Judith, what do you need?"

"Huh? I don't need anything," I said.

"You rang your bell," she said.

"No, I didn't, I'm still sleeping," I laughed.

"Yes, you did. You rang it just a little bit ago," she said.

"No, I didn't," I said a little more firmly. "I'm just about to get up and get ready for the day."

"Okay," she said. "I must have misheard."

"Yes," I said.

Later that day, Carolyn arrived to check in and found that we had a new security system in place.

"Whose idea was this?" she asked.

"It was Linda's idea and I agreed," I said.

"Why? This is a nice neighborhood. It sends the wrong message," Carolyn said.

"Because things were coming up missing," I said. "Did you know someone took Olivia's picture right off the mantle? Who would do that? I'm scared, Carolyn. The security system makes me feel safe."

"Aren't you the one that said that those things probably just got misplaced and that we'd find them in another room?" Carolyn asked.

"I was trying to be optimistic," I said. "But when Olivia's picture went missing, it really scared me."

"Scared you enough to spend hundreds of dollars on a security system?"

"Yes!" I said.

"Well, okay," she said. "I need to talk with Linda about how things are going here."

She and Linda went into the kitchen to talk and I stayed in the front room. I really wished I could hear what they were saying and strained my ear toward the kitchen as best I could, but couldn't make out a thing. A part of me wanted to walk into the dining room so I could hear them, but that would be too obvious. I could only guess what they were saying about me.

When Linda and Carolyn came out, their faces looked pretty grim.

"Mom, Linda says she can still take care of you here, but that she has noticed there are times you are forgetting things," Carolyn said. "I told her how important it is that you take your medication every day and she said she understands and has been giving it to you as prescribed."

"What am I forgetting?" I asked.

"Just earlier today, you forgot that you rang the bell for me," Linda said.

"But I didn't ring the bell," I said.

Linda and Carolyn looked at each other.

I sighed. It felt like the two of them were ganging up on me. I decided to give it up.

"Mom, we're just concerned, that's all," Carolyn said. "Let's go in the kitchen and have lunch."

The three of us headed into the kitchen, where Linda was planning to make sandwiches and chips. As we all got to talking, Carolyn stared off toward the kitchen countertop.

"Mom, did you put away the pressure cooker?" Carolyn asked.

We always left it sit out on the counter because it was so big and didn't fit in any of the cupboards.

"No," I said, looking over to where we stored the pressure cooker. It was gone! Even after we had installed the security system, it was still missing. This was troubling to me.

"Then it's missing," Carolyn said as she opened all the cupboards just to check.

"Maybe it went missing before the guys installed the security system and we just didn't notice," Linda said.

"That could be," I said. I hoped so. What other explanation could there be?

Carolyn did not appear convinced. "Make sure you keep that security system on at all times, even when the two of you are home. Okay?"

"Of course," Linda said.

The next day, Linda said that we needed to go grocery shopping, so naturally, I went with her. We locked up the house, set the security system, and headed out to the grocery store.

Our local grocery store isn't as large as one of the major chain stores, but I still tried to stick with Linda the entire time. This way, I could also point out my favorite foods and menu items for the following weeks ahead. At one point, however, I told Linda I was going to another aisle to get a jar of peanut butter and would be right back. She said okay.

After I found my jar of peanut butter, I walked back to where Linda was, and she was gone! I couldn't believe she moved after I told her I would be right back. I looked in the nearest aisles, and no Linda. Finally, I walked along the end of the rows, looking down each aisle and didn't see Linda in any of the aisles. *Maybe she had gone to the checkout already? She wouldn't have done that knowing that I still had another item, would she?* I didn't want to holler out her name in the store. Finally, I went up to the customer service area and asked them to page her overhead. It was embarrassing, but I couldn't find her anywhere.

"Linda Grime, you have a family member waiting for you at the customer service area. Linda Grime, you have a family member waiting for you at the customer service area," they paged.

Within an instant, Linda was at the customer service area.

"Judith, where have you been? I've been waiting for you right at the place you left me to go get peanut butter."

"No, you weren't. I went back there and you were gone," I said.

"Judith, I was right there," Linda said.

"No, you weren't. I checked every aisle. I was so worried," I said.

"Well, let's not get into it here, at least we found each other and you got your peanut butter. Are we ready to check out and go home?" she asked.

"Yes, I believe so," I said. I was ready to get out of that store immediately.

When we arrived home, Linda typed in the code for the security system, something I was still getting used to, and put the groceries away, while I rested on the sofa in the front room. That had been quite a taxing trip. It surprised me how much energy it had taken out of me. As I was lying down, I happened to notice one of my figurines from a trip Larry and I took to Hawaii was missing off of the end table. It was a glass figurine of a hula dancer.

"Linda!" I called out, instead of using the bell.

"Yes, Judith," she said as she walked into the front room.

"One of my glass figurines is now missing. It's a figurine of a little hula girl from Hawaii. You haven't seen it, have you?" I asked.

"No, I haven't," she said apologetically.

"Where are all of my things going?" I asked, not expecting an answer.

The next day, Carolyn and Cindy came over to do some more cleaning, organizing, and sorting, this time in Cindy's old room. We all pitched in to help and started off first by putting clothes in bags to donate and give away. We found a bunch of old notebooks to throw away. We also found a stash of books to donate. Cindy was looking for one thing, however, and couldn't find it.

"It was hanging right here," she said, pointing to her vanity.

"What are you looking for?" I asked

"Oh, don't you remember?" She asked. "When I was a junior in high school, I won that writing contest and they gave me a medal. The medal was hanging right here, on my vanity."

"Are you sure you didn't put it in a box or something one day?" Carolyn asked.

"I'm sure."

"Well, here's another item to add to the mysterious missing items list," I said. "It just keeps growing."

"Yeah, mysteriously," Carolyn said.

"What does that mean?" I asked.

"It means there's got to be an explanation to all of this," Carolyn said. "And soon we're going to get to the bottom of it."

Chapter 26

Linda was a good caregiver for me overall. Whenever I got upset about something, she had a way of making things better. Usually she'd ask me some question about Larry and that would get my mind off of whatever I was upset about. I loved telling her stories about the two of us. She'd want to know how we first started dating, where our first date was, who said "I love you" first, how he proposed, what life was like with the two girls, and so on. I filled her head with stories of our life together.

She said she loved hearing every bit of it. She said she didn't have much of a story to give me in return. Her ex-husband wasn't much of a companion and, therefore, didn't make for happy story telling. She said she had longed for a relationship like Larry's and mine, but it just wasn't meant to be.

"There's still time," I said. "Don't give up hope just yet."

Linda laughed, "I'm in my sixties. I'm too old for dating."

"You never know when the right man might just sweep you off your feet," I said.

Linda laughed again, "I won't keep my hopes up."

Then, Linda changed the subject, "How about a visit to Pine Meadows today? You said you wanted to visit your friends."

I did tell them I'd come visit. And I probably should. The truth is, I really didn't want to go back to Pine Meadows. I didn't want to think about the place at all, but I did miss Ila, Denise, and Pat. "Yes, that's a good idea, let's go visit."

So, we headed to Pine Meadows. When we arrived, Linda and I checked in as visitors. Linda said she would wait in the front room area as I began my search for Ila and Denise. I had a hunch they'd be in activities at this time, and I was right. Luckily, Kathy let me in to visit with them during balloon volleyball.

"How are you both?" I asked.

"Good," Ila answered.

"The same as always," Denise said, half laughing. "It's good to see you. I didn't think you'd ever come back, honestly. How are you?"

"I'm good. Things are going good at home. Linda's a good caregiver. I get to sleep upstairs in my own bed that Larry and I shared. I can get up and move whenever I want to, with the exception of the stairs. I still need help with those."

"But," Denise said.

"But, what?" I asked.

"There's something in your voice," she said. "Something indicating that all is not well."

"Well, something odd is happening," I said.

"Like what?" she asked.

"Like things are coming up missing in the house frequently. Items come up missing for no reason," I said. "We even installed a security system to keep intruders from coming in and taking things and items are still coming up missing."

"Do you think Linda is taking them?" Denise asked.

I gasped, "That thought never even crossed my mind. I would never dream to blame her."

"Who else could it be?" Denise asked.

"It could still be an intruder," I said. "Someone who learned the code or knows how to bypass security codes."

"Highly unlikely," Denise said.

"I don't think it's Linda," I said.

"You're too trusting," Denise said.

"It could be anyone," Ila said.

We chatted for a few more minutes about life both inside Pine Meadows and outside. It still wasn't the same without Anna. Ila and Denise told me Pat was sitting outside enjoying the weather, so after our visit, I made my way out to the front patio.

"Well, hello there," he said when he saw me.

"Hello Pat, how are you doing?" I asked.

"I'm doing alright, about the same as usual," he said. "The real question is, how are you doing?"

I told him how things were going at home, how much I was enjoying my new-found freedom, and that I found Linda to be an excellent caregiver.

"That's wonderful," he said. "I'm glad to hear things are going so well for you."

"There's just one thing," I said, as I told him about the items that have been going missing around the house. I told him that we installed the security system and that items have still been going missing. I figured if anyone would give me a fair assessment of the situation, it would be Pat.

"That's really unusual," Pat said.

"Yes, it's pretty unnerving as well. Even with the security system, I'm worried about an intruder getting into the house and taking things. I just wonder why he or she is taking such random items?"

"It's just you and Linda in the house?" Pat asked.

"Yes," I answered. I cringed, waiting for him to accuse Linda.

"Hmm," he said. "That is odd. I hope the mystery gets solved soon."

Pat was such a gentleman. That's one of the big reasons why I considered him such a good friend.

After our visit, I said hello to a few of the staff members and a few other residents at Pine Meadows before Linda and I left for the day.

When we returned home, I couldn't help but dwell on my conversation with Denise. It really bothered me. *Could it really be Linda taking the items that were missing in the house? If so, why?* I didn't even want to think about it, but I also didn't want to think about an intruder coming into the house either. Maybe Carolyn and Cindy were just misplacing things when they were re-organizing and forgetting about it. That made the most sense to me. I would have to sit down and talk with them the next time they came over and ask them to be more careful.

It turned out I got my opportunity the very next day. Carolyn and Cindy arrived to do more cleaning and organizing. I asked to speak with them in the front room before we got started. Linda was busy in the kitchen preparing lunch for later.

"Girls, I'm concerned that maybe you're not being careful enough with the re-organization process and that's why we have things turning up missing," I said. "I think if we just try to move a little slower and take our time, we'll have better luck."

"You think the missing items are our fault?" Carolyn asked.

"I don't think it's anyone's fault, I just think if we go about this process a little more carefully, we might find less items coming up missing," I said.

"Mom, we don't think it's the cleaning process," Cindy said.

"What do you think it is?" I asked.

Carolyn and Cindy looked at each other like they were afraid to tell me.

"Mom, can't you see that Linda is taking our things?" Carolyn asked. "I can't explain why she's taking such random items, but it's the only possible explanation. She must be a kleptomaniac, or she has a strange attachment to our things. I don't know."

"No, I don't believe that. It's got to be an intruder," I said.

"Mom, you installed a security system. It would go off if it were an intruder," Cindy said.

"Look, Mom, I'm not saying we have to confront Linda just yet, but if bigger things start coming up missing, we might have to say something," Carolyn said.

I didn't want to believe what I was hearing, but it did make sense. The only two people in the house most of the time were Linda and me. But why would Linda be taking our things? If she wanted something, all she had to do was ask, and I would give her whatever I could.

"How was your trip to Pine Meadows yesterday?" Carolyn asked, changing the subject.

"My what?" I asked.

"Your visit to Pine Meadows to see your friends," she clarified.

I didn't have the faintest idea what she was talking about, so I just responded, "It was fine."

"Just fine?" Cindy asked.

"Yes, it was just fine," I retorted.

At that point, Linda made her way into the front room to let us know that lunch was ready and we all settled into the dining room to eat. As we were passing dishes around, Cindy noticed that one of the glass pitchers was missing from the niche in the wall where it was displayed. There used to be two, but now there was only one.

"No sense looking for it, it'll be as missing as the rest of them," Carolyn frowned.

"I'll still keep an eye out for it today," Linda said.

I was devastated. Larry and I received those pitchers as a gift from our grandchildren just two Christmases ago. They were special. That's why they were proudly displayed in the dining room. I could only pray that the other one would show up again.

"We should make a list of all the missing items in case we need to get the police involved," Cindy said.

"That's actually a really good idea, Cin. I'll get started on that now," Carolyn said.

Linda and I cleared the table as Carolyn and Cindy worked on the list. I looked over at Linda to see if I could detect any worry on her face, but there was none that I noted. I still found it hard to believe that she could do such a thing. But who else could get in beyond the security system?

The next morning, I woke up in an unfamiliar place. The bed was too big and the room was unusually large. I couldn't find my call light. I was scared. I looked all around. Usually, they clipped my call light to my blankets so that it didn't fall on the ground while I was sleeping. It must have fallen underneath the bed, but I wasn't allowed to look by myself.

I searched on top of the bed for my call light. It was nowhere to be found. I searched the new nightstand and found a bell. *Maybe if I rang the bell, someone would come help me? And tell me where I was?* It was my only hope.

I rang the bell as loud as I could.

Someone did come in, a nice-looking woman, dressed in street clothes. I must not be at Pine Meadows anymore, because they all wore uniforms.

"What can I do for you, Judith?" she asked.

She knew my name. I must have been here for a while.

"Where am I?" I asked.

She laughed.

I started to cry. "Where am I?" I asked again.

She stopped laughing, "Oh my, Judith, I'm sorry. I thought you were kidding. Judith, you're home. You're at your house that you used to share with Larry."

I thought about Larry for a moment. He was my husband, I knew that. He was a good man, always treated me well.

"This is the room that you used to share with Larry before he passed away," the woman said.

Larry passed away. I knew that too. It was starting to come back to me.

"This is my home?" I asked the woman.

"Yes," she said. "You worked very hard to leave Pine Meadows and come back here to live."

"And who are you?" I asked.

Her face fell, "I'm Linda Grime. I'm the daughter you gave up for adoption when you were sixteen. We recently made connections again and you invited me into your home to be your caregiver after you left Pine Meadows."

"Oh," I said. "I remember now. We wrote letters."

"Yes, we wrote letters," she said with a smile.

"Do I have other children?" I asked.

Her eyes widened, "Yes, Judith, you do. You have an older daughter named Carolyn and a younger daughter named Cindy."

"Where's my call button?" I asked.

"You don't have a call button here at your house. You use the bell to get hold of me if you need anything. Just keep it in your walker basket," Linda said.

"Oh, okay," I said, "Well, I need to use the restroom."

"You've been taking yourself to the restroom," Linda said.

"I have?" I asked.

"Yes, you do everything yourself except walk up and down the stairs," she said.

"Okay," I said. "But there's one problem. Where is the restroom?"

Chapter 27

Linda spent the next hour giving me a tour of my house. We went through every room, including Carolyn and Cindy's old bedrooms. She guided me up and down the steps and showed me why I needed to have someone with me at all times when going up and down. She gave me a tour of the downstairs rooms and things started to look a bit more familiar.

After our tour, Linda pulled out a photo album and suggested I look through it. It was a large, thick photo album. I opened it to the first page and didn't have the slightest idea who the people were. Linda told me that I had gone through the album with her before and she could tell me who the people were if I wanted, so we sat down and Linda went through and told me who each person was in the photo album.

After that, Linda suggested that we call Carolyn and Cindy to come over for a visit so that I could see them in person. I gladly agreed. I wanted to see my other two daughters.

So, Linda called the girls and they were over at once, both appearing worried.

"Hey, Mom, how's it going today?" one of them asked.

"It's going good. Linda and I are just going through some old photo albums. Now you are … Carolyn?" I asked

"That's right, Mom," she said with a frown.

The other one had tears in her eyes.

"Don't cry, Cindy, I'm just a little forgetful today," I said with a laugh.

She didn't laugh with me, "Do you remember the boys?" she asked.

"Of course, I do," I said, although I wasn't sure what boys she was talking about. I just wanted to make her feel better.

"So, you just woke up today and didn't know where you were?" Carolyn asked.

"Yes," I said. "But thank goodness for Linda. She helped me get things straightened out."

"I still think a visit to the doctor is necessary," Carolyn said.

I could tell Carolyn must be the bossy one.

"But I feel fine now," I said.

"You're not fine," Carolyn said. "You're not your usual self. I think we can all tell that," she said, looking around the room.

Everyone nodded.

So, Carolyn called the doctor and made an appointment for the following day with Dr. Stanbery regarding my forgetfulness.

The following day, I woke feeling refreshed and ready for the day. I got up and started getting around when Linda came upstairs to check on me.

"Is everything okay, Judith?" she asked.

"Yes, why wouldn't it be?" I asked.

"I was just checking after yesterday," she said.

"Why? What happened yesterday?' I asked.

She didn't answer.

I knew I had a doctor's appointment at eleven o'clock, so I finished getting ready and then waited for Linda at the top of the staircase to walk downstairs. We headed down together, ate breakfast, and waited for Carolyn to pick us up.

When Carolyn arrived, Linda and I got in the car.

"How's today?" Carolyn asked.

"Like nothing happened at all," Linda said.

"What do you mean?" I asked.

"Mom, we're going to the doctor because you had an episode yesterday, an episode of forgetfulness. And we want to know what Dr. Stanbery thinks about it," Carolyn said.

I didn't recall having any such episode, however, I didn't recall too much of yesterday at all, so I kept my mouth shut.

We waited in the waiting room for a while, and when we actually made it back to see the doctor, I was surprised he didn't put me through the memory test again.

"So, tell me about this episode that happened yesterday," he said.

Linda proceeded to tell him everything that happened from the time I woke up until the end of the day, with me forgetting where I was to forgetting who everyone was to forgetting where everything was located in my home. She told him that even after looking through the photo album it was difficult for me to recognize Carolyn and Cindy. She said the oddest thing of all was that today I seemed back to my normal self.

"This happens sometimes with certain patients …," Dr. Stanbery said.

I could tell he was trying to be careful what he said and how he said it.

"This happens sometimes with patients with progressive dementia," he said. "I believe Judith's dementia is progressing despite the medication we've prescribed."

"What does that mean? What do we do at this point?" Carolyn asked.

"I'm afraid there's not much else we can do," Dr. Stanbery said. "We've already tried the medication, that was pretty much our last option."

"You mean there's nothing we can do to try to prevent this?" Carolyn asked.

"There's nothing medically that can be done, I'm sorry. There are things like keep her in a familiar environment, a healthy diet, keep family photos around, telling family stories frequently, things like that that might help, but that's about all I can offer to you," Dr. Stanbery said. "Also, if it gets to be too much to handle at home, there's always the option of Pine Meadows again."

"No, thank you," I said.

When we left Dr. Stanbery's office, I could tell Carolyn was upset. She drove Linda and me back to the house without saying a word. When we got back to the house, Carolyn came in with us.

"Are you sure you're going to be able to handle Mom if she has another episode like she did yesterday?" Carolyn asked Linda.

"Of course I can. We handled it just fine yesterday and she and I got through it," Linda said.

"Yeah, but the next time might be much worse," Carolyn said. "I'm just wondering if maybe Cindy and I should step in and take some of the burden off of you."

"There's no need for that," Linda said. "We're doing just fine. I can handle whatever she throws my way, right Judith?" she smiled.

I smiled back. I wasn't planning on causing this much trouble between my daughters, however. "Carolyn, it's really okay. We've been getting along just fine."

"I just don't want anything to happen to you, Mom," Carolyn said.

"Why would anything happen to her?" Linda asked defensively.

"I don't know. Why would anything happen to all of the items in our house that keep going missing, Linda?" Carolyn's tone went cool.

"Wait, are you accusing me of taking the items that have come up missing?" Linda asked.

"Where else could they have gone, Linda? You guys installed a security system and things are still coming up missing. You and Mom are the only ones in the house," Carolyn said.

"But that's just it, the security system was my idea. Why would I offer to install it if I was the one stealing items?" Linda asked. "I don't appreciate being accused, and if I didn't care about Judith so much, I'd walk out that door right now."

"Cindy and I don't care so much about the items. It's more of a trust issue. We want to be able to trust you," Carolyn said.

"You can trust me. I'm not stealing anything from you."

I could tell that Carolyn didn't believe her. Carolyn never did hide her facial expressions well, and this one was a look of distrust and cynicism.

"Cindy and I have had a discussion and we are going to install security cameras throughout the house. It's the only way to figure out who's really taking these items from us."

Linda hung her head, but said nothing.

"Come on Carolyn, do you really think that's necessary?" I asked.

"Mother, think of the things of yours that have been taken," she said. "Don't you want to figure out who's taken them and potentially get them back?"

"I want them back, yes." I really didn't want to admit that I, too, thought that Linda might be the one taking the items.

"Then we need to set up security cameras in every room," Carolyn said. "And that's final."

The following day, Carolyn arrived at the house with a young man from the security camera company to install the cameras. He said he would have it done in a flash. He installed each camera high up in the corner of each room so that it could capture as much of the room as possible. He even installed motion-sensing cameras that would follow any motion detected in the room. Carolyn must have paid him a lot of money.

After he left, Carolyn was sure to inform us how pricey the cameras and the installation were and that we were not to mess with or alter any of the cameras in any of the rooms.

"Do not put duct tape on any of the camera lenses," she said, looking at us both.

"Why would we do such a thing?" I asked.

"I'm just making a statement," she said before she left.

A couple of days later, the girls came over again for a clean-up day and for lunch together. As usual, Linda was busy preparing lunch while the girls and I worked on cleaning up, this time in one of the spare bedrooms upstairs.

As we were sorting through items to donate, give away, or throw away, Cindy started frantically looking around the room for something.

"What's wrong, Cin?" I asked.

"I can't find the box that had my old Barbies in, you know, the ones I kept in their boxes so that they'd be collectables one day?"

"Are you sure they're not back in your bedroom?" Carolyn asked.

"I'm sure. We already went through my bedroom, remember? I'm sure I kept them in here."

"Let's keep looking and see if they turn up. There's a lot of stuff in here," Carolyn said.

But as we continued sorting, we didn't find the Barbies. I knew they were important to Cindy. All throughout her childhood, she wanted to play with them, and I told her they would be more special if we left them in the box. She didn't understand at the time, but as an adult she had grown to understand their value and had kept them all together in a box in the spare bedroom.

"I can't believe Linda would be so bold. She knows there's a camera in here," Carolyn said.

"I still don't want to believe it's her, Carolyn," I said.

"Who else could it be, Mother? A ghost? No one's intruding. You've got your security system on all the time. There's no one else it could possibly be," Carolyn said.

"Please just don't confront her at lunch. She's worked hard to make it for us," I said.

"How long am I supposed to let this go on?" Carolyn asked.

"Maybe just wait until after the meal," I said.

"Okay, fine," she responded.

We went downstairs for lunch that Linda had prepared. I felt guilty eating it, knowing that Carolyn was about to confront her about the missing Barbies and note that it was likely on the security footage. *If it was, in fact, Linda who was taking the items, why would she be so bold as to take something right in front of a security camera?* It made no sense to me.

After lunch, Carolyn started her interrogation.

"Linda, as you know, we were cleaning the upstairs spare bedroom."

"Yes," Linda said.

"Cindy had a collection of rare Barbie dolls, still in their boxes, that she kept in that room. The collection is now missing. Do you know anything about that?"

Linda sighed, "No, Carolyn, I don't know anything about that."

Carolyn pinched the bridge of her nose, "Look, we have security footage in every room—"

"Then let's watch the security footage from every room!" Linda cried out as she threw her hands up in the air.

Carolyn's eyes widened. She wasn't expecting that response out of Linda. "Okay, let's watch the footage," she said.

Carolyn went out to her car and brought her laptop in. She said that was the only way we could watch the footage from the security cameras. She then went upstairs to the spare bedroom and popped out a small chip from the camera. She inserted the small chip into her laptop and a picture popped up of what the bedroom looked like currently. She said she'd have to re-wind it a few days.

We all watched as Carolyn rewound the tape. We saw Carolyn, Cindy, and I cleaning and re-organizing backward, which was kind of funny to watch, and then just a bunch of stillness. However, the tape got to a point where a figure was in the room, removing the box. Carolyn let it rewind up until the point right before that the figure came into the room. Then she pressed play.

We all hovered around the laptop screen to see who the person was. As the person entered the room, I could tell immediately it wasn't Linda. The person was much too old. As I watched the video, Linda, Carolyn, and Cindy all turned to look at me. That's when I realized it: the person in the video was me.

Chapter 28

"Mom … it was you?" Cindy asked.

"I … I don't know," I said. "I don't remember."

"What do you mean, you don't remember?" Carolyn asked.

"I don't remember doing that, what's on the video. I don't remember that," I said.

"Are you just taking things and moving them?" Cindy asked.

"I don't know!" I started to cry.

"This could be a part of her dementia," Linda chipped in.

As Linda started to speak, Carolyn realized she owed her a big apology, "Linda I'm so sorry we blamed you for the items coming up missing. I guess we never would have dreamed that Mom could have done it herself. I'm really sorry."

Linda thought about it for a bit. "It's alright. I suppose that would be your only logical conclusion. I'm just glad we got it straightened out, and hopefully we can find where all those items are located."

"Mom, do you have any idea where you put the items?" Carolyn asked.

"No," I cried.

Linda put her arm around me, "Don't cry, Judith. It's okay."

"Okay, I know another way we can go about this," Carolyn said. "We can take the chip out of every security camera, watch them all, and try to figure out where she goes with the items."

"That seems like a lot of work," Cindy said.

"Do you want to find your Barbies again or not?" Carolyn asked.

"Okay, let's do it," Cindy said.

So, Carolyn took the chip out of every security camera in the house, and for the rest of the day, watched every single one on her laptop. She finally got to the one of the master bedroom upstairs. She called Cindy, Linda, and me over to watch the video with her.

The video of the master bedroom showed me walking into the room, without my walker, holding onto a box of items. I got down on my hands and knees and placed the items under the bed. Then, using the bed as leverage to get back up on my hands and feet, I reached for my walker and went about my day as if nothing had happened.

"All of the missing items must be under the bed!" Carolyn cried out.

We all headed up the stairs, with Linda assisting me, to the master bedroom. Sure enough, as soon as Linda and I arrived, Carolyn was pulling out item after item of what had gone missing in the house. I was both relieved and ashamed. *I couldn't possibly have been responsible for this, could I?* But I was thankful my items had been found.

"Oh, Mother," Carolyn said. "I just don't know how you could have done this. Watching that video, what if you would have broken a hip or something sneaking around like that?"

"I'm fine," I said.

"But you might not have been," Cindy said.

"I think this is obviously getting to be a little bit too much for Linda to handle on her own here," Carolyn said.

Linda didn't say anything.

"What does that mean?" I asked.

"It means we might have to think about Pine Meadows again," Carolyn said.

"Oh, please, no, Carolyn, please. I can't help it that I took the items. I don't know why or what happened, but please let me stay here with Linda. We could hire some extra caregivers if you want to, but please don't send me back to Pine Meadows," I said.

"Mom, watching that video footage, you were doing some pretty risky things, sneaking around behind Linda's back. Your dementia is going to make you do that again. I just don't want anything to happen to you. I think Pine Meadows is the best option. I'm sorry."

I started crying. Linda put her arm around me.

"Please don't do this, Carolyn," I begged.

"Mother, what other option do we have?" she asked.

"Give me another chance, please?" I asked.

"Mother, Dr. Stanbery said you have dementia. This is out of your control. It's not a matter of giving you another chance. Something like this is going to happen again no matter what," Carolyn said.

"It's not fair!" I cried.

"I know it doesn't seem fair, but it has to be done," Carolyn said. "We have to get you back in at Pine Meadows, I'm sorry."

"I'll come visit you every day," Linda said.

"Where are you going to live?" I asked.

"I'll find a place," she said with a smile. "Don't worry about me."

"I'm going to call Pine Meadows in the morning to see if they have a bed available," Carolyn said. "If they do, we're taking it."

I wanted to glare at her, but I knew she was trying to do what was best for me. I wanted to live at home and I had failed. Without even knowing it, I had failed. It didn't seem fair. It was like they gave me a test when I wasn't looking. I'd have to go back and admit to Denise, Ila, and Pat that I couldn't make it at home, even with Linda's help all the time.

That evening, Linda and I packed up my things just in case. It was the second time I'd packed, so I was pretty well used to it. This time, I wouldn't need to pack the lock box, however, because I'd be seeing my baby girl every day. I still wanted to pack Larry's pocket watch. I gathered up all of the family photos that we'd hung on the wall last time, and this time added a few of Linda to hang also. I asked Linda to pack my formal gown also, just in case another prom came up soon.

After we finished packing, Linda and I sat down to a cup of tea before bedtime. I thanked her for everything she'd done for me, caring for me every day for the last several weeks and I apologized for messing it all up.

"You didn't mess anything up, Judith," she said.

"Yes, I did, we had a good thing going here, and then the girls blamed you for stealing our things, and then it turns out I was going behind everyone's back. I'm so sorry," I said.

"It's not your fault, Judith," she said. "Please stop apologizing, okay?"

We hugged each other, knowing that things would never be the same again.

The next morning, Carolyn arrived to the house to announce that Pine Meadows did have a bed available and we were welcome to move in that day.

I had no idea what she was talking about. I turned to Linda for an explanation.

"Judith, you're going back to Pine Meadows today to live," she said.

"But, why? We were getting along so well here. I don't understand," I said.

Linda looked up at me. "You seem to be forgetting things more often," she said. "And we found out that you were sneaking around the house without your walker and going up and down the steps without my help."

Caroline nodded, "It's too much for Linda to handle Mother. A place like Pine Meadows is best for you."

"How do you know what's best for me?" I cried.

"I just don't want to see anything happen to you, Mom. You could have fallen down the stairs, broken a hip, or worse during all of this. They'll keep an eye on you at Pine Meadows, and make sure none of that happens," Carolyn said.

"What if I promise to do better here?" I asked.

"It's out of your control, Mother. Dr. Stanbery says you have dementia, which means a lot of what you're doing, you have no control over," Carolyn said.

I started to cry. I didn't want to have dementia.

Linda hugged me, "Remember, I said I would come visit you every day. I meant that."

So, Carolyn, Linda, and I loaded up Carolyn's SUV with all of the items that we had packed the night before and headed over to Pine Meadows. I cried the entire drive. I had failed living at home.

Joanna met us at the door and said she would show us to my new room, room number 404-B. She said my new roommate's name was Florence. Joanna asked if I remembered all the rules from before, or if I needed an aide to come down and explain everything. I told her I remembered all the rules.

When we got to the room, it looked exactly the same as my previous room: small and drab. Linda and Carolyn got to work right away on fixing it up to look more like home, while I sat in the recliner provided by the facility. I wasn't allowed to get up and help without using my call light for assistance, and knowing how busy the aides were at this particular time of day, I decided to let Carolyn and Linda do most of the work.

As the girls were setting things up, I heard someone say "knock knock" and pull back the curtain. It was my new roommate, without an aide! I didn't know how long she'd been here, but surely, she had to know the policy by now.

"Hello, dear, I just wanted to introduce myself. My name is Florence," she said.

"Hello, it's nice to meet you. I'm Judith," I said. "And these are my daughters, Linda and Carolyn."

"It's nice to meet you all," she said.

"Pardon me for asking, but where's your aide?" I asked.

"Oh, dear," she laughed. "I'm independent."

"What does that mean?" Carolyn asked.

"I went through a round of therapy here and, at the end, the therapist told me I could be independent in my room, meaning I could get up as I pleased to use the restroom and get about in my room. I still have to use my call light to go out into the hallways, but oh, what freedom!" she said with a smile.

"That's wonderful!" I said.

I thought to myself, *I never did finish my first round of therapy here before I left. What if I finished a round of therapy and they told me the same thing? It would be wonderful to be able to get up and about in my room without having to use my call button, especially to be able to use the restroom without having to call for help.*

"Are you still allowed to call for help if you need it?" Carolyn asked Florence.

"Oh, of course. I still do, especially at night time," she responded.

"That sounds like a good goal, Judith," Linda said.

"Your daughters are doing a delightful job of decorating your room, Judith," Florence said. "It looks like you have a lovely family," she gestured over to the photographs going up on the wall. "Once you have your independence, you'll have to come over and see mine."

"I promise I will do that," I said. And I meant it.

Once Florence left to go back to her room, the girls finished up putting everything in place and sat down on the bed to talk for a while before getting ready to leave. I made Linda promise again that she would come to visit me every day. She, of course, said that she would. Pine Meadows was a very lonely place without visitors, so her promise meant a lot.

Then they left. And I cried until dinnertime.

When the aide, Kristi, came to get me for dinner, my spirits had perked back up a little bit. Not just because I recognized Kristi, but because I knew I'd be seeing Ila and Denise at dinner. I prayed there would be a place for me to sit by them.

When we arrived, I asked Kristi to park me at our usual table. Neither Denise nor Ila had arrived yet. When they finally did, they both looked at me in shock.

"What are you doing here?" Denise asked.

"I'm back," I said.

"Back as in …" Ila trailed off.

"I'm back, as in I moved back in," I said.

"What happened?" Denise asked.

"Well, I guess I have dementia, and it comes and goes. At home, I was doing some things that were out of character and going behind Linda's back to go upstairs on my own. That worried the girls, so they sent me back here," I said.

"Oh, I'm so sorry Judith," Ila said.

"At least I have you two. And my new roommate seems nice. Did you know that therapy can make you independent in your room?" I asked.

"Yes, I've just never graduated from therapy," Denise said.

"I never have either," Ila said.

"I didn't know that until Florence came over and told me. I'm going to try to graduate from therapy and become independent in my room. It sure would make things a little bit more tolerable around here."

"If anyone can do it, you can," Denise said.

The following day was a therapy day and I was as excited as ever. I couldn't wait to tell my therapist my goal of becoming independent in my room. It turned out my therapist was Jill again, because she would need to do a new evaluation on me since I had been gone for a while.

At this point, I was pretty used to the routine of the evaluation: balance tests, strength tests, watching me walk. She took notes. Then she explained again that I would likely be working with Rob for most of my therapy sessions, but occasionally may work with a different therapist. I didn't know whether to bring up to her or to Rob that I wanted to be independent in my room, but I figured now was as good of a time as ever.

"Uh, Jill, I'd really like to be independent in my room by the time my therapy is over. Could we make that a goal?" I asked.

"Sure!" she answered. "I think that's a very feasible goal. I'll be sure to let Rob know what we're working toward."

Soon, Rob came out to work with me and go through the exercises. He put me through a lot of balance challenges, knowing that if I was on my own in my room I might drop something and need to pick it up. He also had me do a lot of reaching tasks and stepping. He told me I was doing great. Rob also had me practice pulling curtains back and opening heavy doorways to simulate opening the curtains and doorway to the restroom in my room. He told me he didn't think it would be too long until I could be independent in my room.

At two o'clock that afternoon, we had activities. Wouldn't you know it, it was Skip-Bo. Of course, I asked my aide to assist me over to where Pat was sitting, as I still wasn't entirely sure how to play the game. Pat seemed genuinely surprised and happy to see me.

"Hey there, young lady, what are you doing here?" he asked.

"My family sent me back," I said.

"Why's that?" he asked.

"My doctor says I have dementia," I shuddered at the word. "And I guess I was doing some things that were out of character at home that worried my daughters. They were worried I might fall or potentially break a hip going up and down the stairs by myself, so they decided I should come back here to live."

"What about Linda?" he asked.

"She said she's going to find a place to live in the area. She promised to come visit me every day. She should be here any time now," I said.

"It's good that she's going to stay in the area," he said.

"Yes, I am blessed," I said.

"Well, I'm sorry to see that you had to come back, but I am glad to see you," Pat said with a smile.

"Thank you," I said, blushing.

And as we played Skip-Bo, he was the perfect gentleman like always, assisting me with my cards, not worrying about beating me, and just laughing and having a good time.

After Skip-Bo, Linda was waiting outside of the activities room to take me back to my room for a visit, just like she had promised. She pushed me in my wheelchair, which was allowed, down to my room, and then we called for an aide to assist me into my recliner.

"So, how has everything been going?" Linda asked.

"It's not like home, with you," I said, tears forming in my eyes.

"Did you re-connect with your friends?" she asked.

"Oh yes, that was wonderful. They were surprised and happy to see me. It was like I'd never left to them," I said.

"What about Pat?" she asked.

"Pat was the same as always, still a gentleman," I said.

"Well that's good," she said. "At least your good friends are still here and you've re-connected with them."

"I did therapy today," I told her.

"Oh yeah? How did that go?" Linda asked.

"It went really well," I told her. "The therapists both said it was a feasible goal for me to become independent in my room. We did a lot of exercises and simulations today to replicate what it would be like for me to be independent in my room. Rob said I did a pretty good job."

"That's wonderful!" Linda said. "I'll be praying that it all works out."

"Have you had any luck finding a place to live yet?" I asked.

The market in Bedford Hills wasn't exactly booming, but there was plenty of real estate. I didn't know what Linda's financial situation was, but if it was average, she should be able to find a modest home or nice-sized apartment without much trouble. I hoped she meant what she said when she said she planned to stay in town.

"Well, actually, I've talked with Carolyn and Cindy. And I think I'm going to buy the house, you know, keep it in the family, if that's all right with you of course," Linda said.

I felt the tears well up in my eyes. I couldn't have been happier, "Oh Linda, that makes me so thrilled. I was so afraid the house was going to get sold at an auction to a stranger. Knowing that you'll be living there, gives me so much more peace of mind," I said.

"I'm so glad you feel that way, Judith!"

"And, one more thing, when you're ready, if you're ever ready, please feel free to start calling me 'Mom' like the other girls. You're my daughter just the same," I said. I didn't want to pressure her. I didn't raise her, but I loved her just as much as I loved Carolyn and Cindy.

"Okay, Mom," she said with a smile.

We gave each other a hug.

A couple of weeks later, I had pretty much settled in to Pine Meadows. I spent a lot of time with Ila and Denise, many afternoons on the front patio with Pat, and I had finally done enough therapies to graduate and become independent in my room. Florence and I had grown to become great friends, which really began the day I walked over to say hello and check out her room.

"Knock knock," I said, in the same style she had said to me when she came over to my room on my first day back.

"You're independent! Come on in!" she said with a smile.

I walked into her room and noticed she had many more photos on her wall than I did.

"Wow, how many children and grandchildren do you have?" I asked in wonder.

She smiled, "I have six children, eighteen grandchildren, and eight great-grandchildren."

"Wow, you must be so proud," I said. "Congratulations."

"Thank you," she said.

"Would you like to play a game of Tripoly?" she asked.

"I sure would," I replied.

I knew that spending time with Florence would turn out to be a wonderful friendship.

All of the girls came to visit in those weeks following my initial move back to Pine Meadows. Carolyn, Cindy, and Linda—who had come to visit every day—all came for a visit on a Saturday afternoon when things were a little slower at the Meadows.

"How are you feeling about everything, Mom?" Carolyn asked.

"I'm feeling pretty good. I'm glad Linda's buying the house. That way I can still come back and visit. I feel good about being independent in my room. I'm glad I have such good friends here. Florence is a wonderful friend. And I still have Denise and Ila. And Pat." I blushed.

"So, you're okay with being here at Pine Meadows?" Cindy asked.

"Well, of course, there's no place like home. I'd rather be at home. But I understand why I'm here. You had to do what you had to do. I look around and see people who are in far worse shape than I am, and I realize how blessed I am," I said.

"That's one way of looking at it, Mom," Linda said.

"We just want what's best for you, Mom, and we don't want anything to happen to you. We love you Mom," Carolyn said.

"I love you girls, too," I said.

The four of us hugged each other.

"How about a visit back home? You can see what I've done to the place," Linda suggested.

"That would be wonderful!" I said.

So, Linda checked me out at the front desk, and soon we were on our way back to the house in Bedford Hills. I hadn't been there in weeks, so I was excited.

When we arrived at the house, Carolyn and Linda helped me out of the car and into the house. When I walked in, the place was immaculate. Linda must have done a thorough cleaning.

"Linda this place looks amazing!" I exclaimed.

"Thank you," she said, blushing. "How about I make some lunch?"

"That sounds great," I said.

As I walked around the house, I noticed all of the items that I had hidden under the bed were back in their places. Linda must have done that. She'd also dusted, vacuumed, and spot cleaned every inch of the house. The whole house looked immaculate.

Carolyn, Cindy, and I sat down in the dining room while Linda was making lunch.

"Do you want any help?" Carolyn hollered out toward the kitchen.

"No, thanks! I've got it!" Linda hollered back.

"That woman …" Carolyn laughed.

"So, is it good to be home, Mom?" Cindy asked.

"Oh yes," I said. "It's always good to be home, especially with all my girls."

"I wish we could keep you here, Mom, but you do understand why we can't, right?" Carolyn asked.

"I understand," I said. "I really do."

Pretty soon, Linda came in to the dining room with lunch. As usual, it was grand. We all ate like we hadn't eaten in days and thanked her for the meal. After a bit longer of a visit, it was time to head back to Pine Meadows.

When we returned to Pine Meadows, Linda signed me back in and we all re-convened in my room. This time, it was the girls who acted like they didn't want to leave, rather than me not wanting them to leave.

"What's up girls?" I asked.

"Are you sure you're okay, Mom?" Carolyn asked.

"Of course, I am," I said. "Why?"

"You're usually a lot sadder when we come back here," Cindy said. "This time, you seem, almost, happy."

"I am happy. I got to go home and have a visit with you girls, which I hope to do again sometime soon. I'm in a safe place, where if my dementia acts up, I know I'll be okay. I have good friends here. I'm independent in my room. I have a lot to be thankful for," I said.

"I'm glad you see it that way, Mom," Carolyn said.

"I could have it a lot worse. At least I have all three of you girls," I said.

Epilogue

I miss Larry like nobody's business, first and foremost. I'd give anything to have him back. Things would be so much different if he were still here. But I have to accept the fact that he's not, and I'm learning to. I just pray that he's looking down on me now and smiling because I haven't put up too much of a fight over the choices that have been made for me by our girls. I hope he's as happy as I am that Linda bought our house and is keeping it in the family.

I'm so blessed to have found my baby girl, Linda. Who would have thought she would end up living here in Bedford Hills, in my home? I'm so thankful to the activities department for having us write those letters and to Denise and her daughter for helping me find Linda. It was a long process, but well worth it. I think Larry would have liked to know her too.

I'm so thankful for Carolyn and Cindy. They may be polar opposites, but they're my daughters and I love them more than anything. I don't hold a grudge against Carolyn for putting me in Pine Meadows. She had to do what she thought was best, and I know she just wanted to keep me safe. I think Larry's sudden death had a significant impact on her and Cindy, making them a bit overprotective of me, and that's okay.

I will always treasure my time spent at the house with Linda. She is such a sweetheart for taking on being my caregiver and trying to keep an eye on me. Although I didn't know I was taking things and hiding them, I still wish we could have worked it out that I could have stayed there. But I do understand why it didn't. Dementia has its grip on me, but I intend to fight back with everything I have for as long as I can.

Here at Pine Meadows, things are looking up now that I'm independent in my room. I love the freedom of being able to walk around my room and to be able to take myself to the bathroom when I want to. I also love the freedom of being able to visit Florence whenever I want to. She's a hoot. I just love her. We just chat or play games, anything to pass the time.

Denise and Ila are still my number-one pals. Denise is the outspoken one, since Anna passed away of course, and Ila is still the quiet one. Denise isn't afraid to tell me like it is when I ask for her advice and Ila is always the first to offer to pray for me, and I could certainly use the prayers!

And then there's Pat. Oh, sweet Pat. He's such a lovable guy. Neither one of us is ready for a relationship yet, but I'm so glad he's my friend. He's always right there for me if I need something and always willing to help me play a game of Skip-Bo. And who could forget being king and queen of the prom?

You see, my life is actually pretty good. I have good friends and good family and I wouldn't change them or change my circumstances for anything.

www.ingramcontent.com/pod-product-compliance
Lightning Source LLC
Chambersburg PA
CBHW031044160726
47991CB00005B/2022